AF441223

The world of ghosts and metaphysics

Annalize Michel: The True Story of the Most Famous Haunted Girl

A German girl is young and full of hope: her life suddenly turned into a living hell, when evil spirits made their way past you, and from her soul she wanted it herself, it's me not Michelle, the girl turned into a Saint in the eyes of the mission, fought with the devil and defeated him , come with me, dear readers, let's move on to the world's most popular story of a girl about the reincarnation of her gender.

Nee Annelise... Michelle in one of the cities of the county of Bavaria, Germany in 1952 in a family of practicing Catholics and lived a normal life until the age of sixteen, where she suddenly developed some symptoms of exotic heavy care and lack of control over the movement of some parts of her body, so did her parents inserting her into the hospital for treatment, but her condition continued to deteriorate and I began to see shades of the existence of the strange and hear voices and screams of terror in her head telling her that she would "burn in hell". During the therapy session and said, that I was not her doctor, that her body was a ghost, and it sounds strange, I started ordering her to do some things that I did not want to do, but her doctor explained the words to her, because he was just Hallucinations that made me not lose hopes for medical treatment, but began to pick up in order to receive them through sessions andexorcisms of the church.

Did her pet parents have multiple pastors to do the job and get her gender out, but their request was denied within two times, and this is because church standards allow someone to touch her and one of the most important of these standards or conditions is that a person looks like a strong dislike and disgust for religious symbols or speak a foreign language not he or anyone from his family or any mother or or include the supernatural and strange.

I started a case, I didn't get any worse, he took the curse and
bought her for the family and bit her, trying to get close to her, as I
started to abstain from food because of sex that could prevent her
from doing this, and went to tear her clothes on. and sleep on the
floor, and eat his spiders and flies, and began to scream hysterically
for hours, and break any cross, resting his hand on it, and tear
images of Christ, and break pots of flowers and roses, as she began
to find a community, and spend parts your body, and urinate on
the floor of the room, and drink your urine sometimes.
Due to poor condition, her approved church finally held a hearing
to ask the gender of her body and during 1975-1976 there was a
session or two sessions of weekly ones who told them during these
sessions that her body was possessed by six demons or more from
the Spirit of Cain, as well as Nero and Hitler.

Despite the fact that I did not begin to feel some comfort after the
church meetings, but she never fully healed and constantly suffered
tantrums, very similar to the conflict of freezing her body through
her, as they were paralyzed and fainted, the sex exorcism meetings
continued in the church for several months, and often the same
people were present, two ministries of pastors and a father, I am
not, and sometimes some of the parishioners. Pastors record and
hearings in 40 bars are played for ten months, and if I didn't get out
of hand sometimes through the skin that contains three people, tell
the client to hold it, although its weight did not become about forty
kilograms, and sometimes they were forced to supply her with
chains.

The last session was on July 30, 1976, and his name
was Anneliese . during this period she just suffered from
pneumonia and high temperature, as she became in the middle of
pressure and, as a result of abstaining from food for a long time,
was the last phrase during her last " pleading for forgiveness", and
in the evening of the same day she turned to her mother's swindler

for the last time and said in a trembling voice: "Mom, I'm scared," and these were her last words if she died that very night.

Registration is very rare and the fact of the matter is that it was submitted during trial and sound sex
The police arrested the reason for the two procedures for sex exile meetings and so will be with my parents, I am not accused of negligence leading to death only in the police report, the main reason for me was not hunger was the result of abstaining from food and the police concluded that if you were forced not to eat until the week of her death, you can avoid her death, during the trial she said that she did not choose that her deceased's brother she hated the hospital because they forced her to take medications and also some food was presented cassettes that were recorded during church meetings and that contain several sentences or phrases are strange, for example, the edges, like a mountain between the two genitals, about which he left the body I'm not the first, and they spoke in a manly voice with a strange accent. But the psychiatrist who brought his court to a scientific case, I am not, he said that he was suffering from a case of a severe mental disorder, and he was saved from death if I was brought to the hospital a week before her death, and on this basis the court recognized the parents not guilty as well as guilty shepherds and sentenced him to six months in prison with commentary for each of them.

After her death, I stopped serving saints in the eyes of many and became a grave of benefits for many visitors, as her life and her story became a major problem and several films were made inspired by her story, perhaps the most famous is the USA film "Exorcism of Emily Rose "house in 2005.

Gene and mental illness

The stigma of her mental illness is mainly due to the belief, widespread among ordinary people and most Islamic scholars, that a psychiatric patient in an act of mass murder is either inhabited by a devil or a demon, or at least is under the influence of magic, the evil eye or envy. It helped the media - print, audio and watch without knowing in support of this conviction before the council, so that those who believe in this conviction express their opinions, strongly support those views with Quranic verses and prophetic sayings, and narrations of the Prophet, peace him. It is worth mentioning that there are a few Muslim scholars who do not support this belief when entering the floor of a patient's case, but they are reluctant to voice their opinions for fear of naming their college or dissent.

The ratio of these popular beliefs, there are a large number of psychiatric patients means that the Senate is more than those who are notorious for treating obsessions and removing traces of magic, and they pay big bucks to stop healing in various ways known to these therapists, which we will mention later. ... It is strange that these therapists do not have the means of a specific diagnosis, and instead of affirming any psychological symptoms for each patient, it is generally accepted that she did magic or the evil eye, or envy, or the Devil. Most of the patients who saw psychiatrists reported that they collaborated for a time, when these older people chose to eventually see a psychiatrist, after which their health deteriorated or because they were distinguished, they went astray.

In our society of the East and Islam, it was believed that most psychiatrists do not at all object when they hear the patient's condition, recite the Koran or prayers, because they are sure that these means, which are part of the components of the patient's belief system, help to support and accelerate the medical treatment of the hand of Faith to the cause. God and she desires him with the expectation of answering her prayers and is used to raise the message about them. But it is very important not to interfere with Al- Mutawah or the thing in drug treatment or try to carry out subsequent treatment of the patient or his family, because a large number of them do not believe in any role of students in therapy.

The butler's faith in the devil's closet prevailed in what we now call the developed countries, in the last century, the specific weight of the Church's faith in this matter, except that as a result of the scientific Renaissance, the influence of the Church has decreased, this faith has almost disappeared, and by now she is considered superstitious.

Short story
Faith is the responsibility of evil spirits for any kind of disease, ancient, eternal was among the primitive tribes on the first date, an analysis of epidemics and natural disasters attributed to any tribe's misfortune, as well as to these evil spirits, if not, then at whom their gods were angry and punished their. Accordingly, there the spirits of good, like the spirits of their ancestors, resorted to their own doctors for their inspiration and helped them in getting rid of the misfortunes of evil spirits, saved from the consequences of disasters, epidemics and helped them overcome their enemies.

These were spirits beyond imagination in the "place of the old," just as was the case in "Babylon of the old," it was the priests of certain rituals who expelled these spirits from the bodies of the sick, included prayers and incense, as well as prayers to the gods and sometimes identified these spirits and ordered her out.

Wrote the Hindu Scripture, "I lead", which I placed in a thousand years BC, I also spoke about these evil creatures, and also dealt in Persia in the sixth century BC. The books that go back to these civilizations also speak of the ritual of exorcising these spirits through prayers and holy water.

Stating that "Homer" can meet the devil, "Socrates" has a description of a government that is under the influence of Satan. As confirmed by "Plato" himself.

Roman ritual, the special play of sex and drinking play a big role in it and carry themselves in the net, entering their own vanity. Later it was transferred to Ancient Greece.

Tradition and "shamanism" whether you hold evil spirits and the devil responsible for stealing the patient's life and whether they receive in return his disease renewed, follows from a processor called a "shaman" to search for those souls that are stolen and returned to their owner after the expulsion of the evil spirit for healing the patient.

To this day, we find this belief in the "purchase of spirits" by a product not only in third world countries, but also between groups in developed Western countries who believe in reincarnation, that is, that some spirits of the dead who came into her life or for a moment the paradox of her life, instead of ascending into the sky, they soar above the earth to reach their owner in a new renewed body, experiencing enormous psychological and physical suffering. As a result of this belief, a large number of spiritual healers appeared who attuned these patients to these spirits, to their own rituals. It is worth mentioning that some contemporary psychotherapists carried out a method of psychotherapy called "the sign of the salvation of souls." This treatment is often performed under hypnosis. This is similar to the methods of spiritual healers, which largely depend on the exploitation of the contract to the patient.

Spirit Possession / Spirit Release Therapy

Book of the New Testament
Challenge of the New Testament, a book by Christians that Jesus Christ practiced the ritual of expelling spirits from the patient's body, confirming his prophecy and the Prophet commanding these spirits to leave the patient's body, and I will never return. It has already been said that in his life he made a sick body a herd of pigs that walked without her, which ran to the edge of the cliff and fell into the water to die. It has been argued that Jesus taught his disciples to cast out spirits from the bodies of the sick. This day is available to the church, especially to the Catholic one, it is

important. The Old Testament books said that you know some of
the prophets of the devil.

The Holy Quran emphasizes that one of the miracles of the Prophet
Jesus, peace be upon him, heals the sick, if God willing, with his
prayers he calls him.

Until recently, he was mentally ill in Europe, thought he was a
demon or a witch, hunted them down and killed them, burning
them for them. Finally, they themselves began to deal with the
disappearance of this faith, as they collect funds in private clinics
for their care and protection.

Sex in Islam
It is known that the inhabitants of the Arabian Peninsula before the
advent of Islam, the people of the book, Jews, use and empower
Arab boys, and they themselves believe in the existence of sex and
its influence on a hated and desired person as talentedly as the
customer believes that their criminals who inspire im strongly
fantastic hair. They were assisted by the army in creating pressure,
danger and uncertainty. The Valley of Genius, deciphering the
valley in the Arabian Peninsula, was believed to inhabit her
sex. The word "genius" comes from this name.
The Holy Quran emphasizes the presence of sex, as it says in
Lucifer, which was from the floor, and some verses indicating their
presence, he does not consider as "the cheese that we created
earlier, from the Heavenly fire", but says:
"creating Marj University of fire. "" And they were created before
Adam came, two thousand years ago.

You know the Prophet, peace and blessings of Allah be upon Him,
in his conversations with them he seemed to say: "Show me the
side in which I passed the prayers", and said: "What do you do
alone with your gender partner and his angels. " Remember the
mention of the genital creatures of the chilling chip, since the air

does not see a person, but they see him and have a displacement in the form of friendly and affectionate animals - snakes, scorpions and birds. Whose believer and unbeliever will enter heaven and hell on the day of Resurrection according to their deeds.

Satan disobeyed his Lord, except that Allah Almighty gave him punishment until the day they, and that day, vowed to seduce a person with weak faith and do good to pay him for people.

As the Quran says, the God of sex Sidney Solomon works for him. "Work from sex between his hands with the ear of the Lord." It was also stated that people knew magic and medicine.

The Muslim does not deny the existence of sex, but the differences in the interpretation of this verse: "who ate the Lord, they not only say that Satan flops." This verse is taken as evidence that the project is entering the devil's body, it is failing. Everything that comes from the GTA designer cramps and involuntary movements are weird and fly out of the mouth from opaque words or obscene TV Photos. And also a demonstrated need and three women who do not drive their son crazy, take him for lunch and dinner, so there was a Prophet, peace be upon him only to scan the floor of his belly on his son's chest like a "black puppy". In the case of the second command of the apostle, saying: "Get out the enemy of God," came out.

Devil whisper man
There is a great Muslim belief about the mediation of the devil to man in order to lure him for disobedience to his Lord, and that to his power come "from evil, those who are possessed, etc. Who whisper in the chest of people." Plus, they are interpreted as hidden photos that do not feel entitled to highlight them or toss them hidden into the soul. It is said that OCD often causes dogs to hate confrontation and this leads to epileptiform . They can be compulsive dogs, prone to souls and of course cars and aspirations

that I don't understand, fulfilled the contract. Some books on thinking have said that Satan enters the body of the son of Adam because the body is good or thin lead is not what happens to the very bad ideas that lead to sin. And even though he speaks with the Sheriff "to the devil in the human bloodstream."

Modern science provides yet another explanation for this obsessive suffering of many psychiatric patients who have become devilish, which we will discuss in more detail later in the second part of this article.
Exorcism of the devil by Mars
The belief that sex or the devil leads to conflict or sex has led to the emergence of healers in man, many of whom are more confident in the intention of the honest some as a quick win. Often, the diagnosis is made in bulk if the factory movements and seizures appear vague or dirty, or the seizures are similar to epileptic seizures. If the patient had suspected mental disorders, passion played a prominent role, such as sadness or anxiety, anger or fear, cravings or guilt, lack of confidence or loss of appetite, or sex or pleasure in life or work, the illness is often the result of eyes or magic or work or envy.

The Genie's exit on the date of enrollment has different methods, for example, a man's and a chair verse he read to himself, and it is believed that these methods negatively affect the sex or the Devil and lead to his expulsion from the patient's body. Some psychotherapists resort to direct methods of dealing with stubborn and disturbing Spa , he plays it and is in a hurry to find out why, the United States had its share of the stick, often screaming and screaming underfoot. The belief here is that the original project, it does not feel pain, but sex is a sufferer who often leaves the factory project to win, but can come back again, it requires the master to revise again.

True, every thing is a harmless beating of an injured patient, he personally cries and cries for mercy, but I don't give a damn about that because it is believed that the one who suffers and shouts is a pixie and continues to press to sometimes faint on the patient or have the intelligence of his Vespa his doctor about anything did not ask. Because the patient died as a result of stress or starvation or exposure to natural health hazards.

It is known that some patients, when they, in the absence or change of consciousness as a result of the type of " breakdown or wearing disorder", may not respond to external stimuli, such as pain, it is considered, when the mistake that the lack of response means that sex is the one who is feeling pain, not a patient who seems to have no influence, it is clear what is happening to her at this moment, but you can notice a trace of mischief when they return to full consciousness.

Does Danny agree to phone sex?
The circle of mu and some Muslim communities that deny the entry of sex into the human body is the source of the project for the impossibility of the spirit entering into one body. Among us now there are a number of Muslim scholars of our contemporaries who claim their opinion that they are fearless heretics or infidels.

In this regard, one of them says: "The word to wear or not to wear is contained in the Qur'an or Sunnah. And as it is said in the words of the Almighty," how Satan flops down. " And also the Meaning "I touched me the devil." No entry means sex of my human body, but whispering behind them causes slowdown or epilepsy. A person from his weakness will be amazed when he hears the story that she whispered, including repeating it himself or what makes God angry. "

Note here that in both cases, the devil is responsible for or phase differences in the way the latter group believes that the conflict is the result of Satan's whispers and does not enter the devil for the patient's body.

Witness from her family
A few years ago, one of the Qur'anic healers wrote an article in the newspaper that for many years he had treated patients of the Qur'an with references mainly to wholesale or envy, or the eye, or magic, but when you see books on science, medicine, psychology, make sure that the cases that have been treated are described more accurately in those books and they respond to treatment when the psychiatrist is more comprehensive and faster. And on that day, he called his career forever, and recommended that doctors reconsider it once, because they can diagnose the situation and handle it better. Even if science has advanced in the life of the Prophet, may peace be with him, in the face of patients of the same purpose with the strengthening of medical treatment according to the Quran and prayer. And the same was reported that "the cure for all diseases except the pyramid"

An increasing number of Muslim scholars now believe in mental illness and organic disease and also believe in medical treatment for these diseases in Sudan, many of the elders who had their psychiatric patients in mind have strong relationships with local psychiatrists as they refer their cases to these doctors, and then maintain these drugs and order the patient to take them according to the doctor's advice. This method is very effective, as drug treatment is supported by a religious marriage with the patient's adherence to the treatment regimen.

Of the great scientific achievements of the end of the last century in the Western world, a significant role was played by the decadent belief that reigned there in the butler's closet of the devil-man, who was attacked and mentally or organically ill, inclined to this belief in the church and its followers, and few in the community. Currently, there is a classification of generally accepted descriptions and most of the pathological conditions in which it was believed that the role of the devil in creating him is also now available in medical procedures, varying to control him.

In return, keep this faith in third world countries to this day in proportion to the influence of religious and socio-cultural, as well as follow the scientific Renaissance and poor education, scientific and medical.

The general description that comes around or the Devil is that someone is eccentric and looks abnormal or the body of a word and he is strange or incomprehensible or obscene, or speaking in a foreign language and miraculous power. She is not religious in man and his symbols. He also stated that he can move into his body so that it looks dead or unconscious, to slow down his breathing and his heart, to paralyze the movement of his body and his reaction to external stimuli. He stated that he considered his spasms or uprisings to be muscle movements of surprise or chosen spells of powerful emotions such as anger, trust and pain, and revolves around.

The strangest thing is that most of these symptoms can be previewed in the psychological or nervous or mental state of the patient, but not necessarily the whole community, but according to the medical diagnosis that can be achieved after the disclosure of the medical history, psychological tests, or laboratory work. necessary. I will briefly mention the most important of them within the three classifications.

A - neurological disease:

"Neurological diseases"

Epilepsy:

A common disease among children and what refers to an attack of a large and sharp one, that where he loses consciousness of the patient, and then is chosen by muscle spasms, usually accompanied by muscle uprisings, all-round and released oil, which from his mouth either urinates on himself or cuts his tongue teeth until it populates his body so that the source does not live for several minutes on what happened to her during the seizure. These attacks can be clearly tracked by a mock brain and can be controlled with anti-conflict situations. They may have seizures in later age, since as a result of traumatic brain injury, they can be diagnosed and treated with medication.

Disease de la Tourette "de la Tourtte ":
Here the patient passes from the gadfly to the voice and motor, which sharply causes her severe disorder. A gadfly is a voice or uprising movement whose harshness can inadvertently confuse or frighten the audience. Sometimes the sounds of words, obscene or offensive, are considered to be related to what is meant for the sick person, so you might think that the person is possessed by the devil.

B- mental illness: "mental illness"

Schizophrenia:
Mental illnesses are common knowledge and are easily diagnosed and symptom controlled with antipsychotics. In short, the patient lacks discernment and contact with reality and has faith in what is false or delusional. maybe he is a prophet sent to guide humanity or property, or to reap control of his body and in his movements and actions. Selected hallucinations — auditory or visual — taught her things that didn't exist. Some sufferers have symptoms that put their bodies under prolonged exposure or CHECK their own bodies. Sometimes they enter in the absence of immobility, during which they do not react to any external stimulus, that is, in the case of immobility of the physical whole. And sometimes they are in a

state of excitement that Hogan might destroy or harm people around them. In the playoffs, this is often thought of as being the devil. All cases of schizophrenia are aimed at touching the body.

Mania disease and psychotic depression:
In schizophrenia, it has been reported that the patient may have delusions or hallucinations in addition to the symptoms described. The patient is very depressed or reckless and difficult to control.

C - mental illness: "psychological illness"

Essence disorder is another "identity disorder":
Multiple Personality Disorder was previously known. Talk to the sick entity or with two or more glances from time to time when the patient is under intense psychological pressure or suffers from a case of crying in pain. Everything personal, detached from the hand of perception, thinking, memory, memories and does not include anything about the other personality, and here you might think that a person red-handed when reincarnating his personality is not generally accepted.

Having a transformational "conversion disorder":
In this disorder, a violation of motor function or sensory function is observed, suggesting the presence of a disease and general medical or neurological. It occurs when the patient is suffering from stress or power struggles. Sensory symptoms include loss of sensation or system or palate, war includes spells to select performance, or a semi- epileptic can be interpreted as being caused by a genie or devil.

Having another " dissociative disorder":
Here the patient casts spells where your mental abilities of perception, memory and thinking, as well as your sense of yourself and the situation can be accompanied by movements or spasms

involuntarily and involuntarily, during which the patient's consciousness is disturbed. So you think the bus touch is sex.

Example: A young man sitting between her parents suddenly falls to the ground and has convulsions or chooses the needs of movement, and they are illegible in words, but they are not completely unconscious, but embarrassed and impervious to others. Let you live by muscle movements, but this knowledge can be used in case of distortion of consciousness and thinking for a while. Repeated attacks in different positions. You might think this situation is the result of a wholesale exchange. The fact is that this screen whenever a conflict or psychological pressure is not possible for him or is unable to resolve or cope with the interference in shifting from the side and temporarily to the conflict.

I must point out that this is not a case of epilepsy where the main interaction between them is easily handled by specialists.

Possessing another "trance of possession":
Sometimes the presence of the other above can take a different turn that the patient is thought to be able to decide or reincarnate, and whatever appears is the work of Satan.

These cases show the cultural and religious role of big people, because the community in which they live believes in the sex of the human body. The difference between these cases and schizophrenia is that these cases appear in the patient from time to time, in order to be between them in a natural way, a deformation of consciousness occurs during a seizure. More importantly, there is no apparent deterioration in the patient's professional, social or personal characteristics between shifts.

Remember in this area that the Omani family and I led my young daughter to sex, populated from time to time, being struck by a living being to his senses and rising all over her body and speaking her language. They took her to a local resident, who confirmed that she was being chased by Pound, but was unable to get it out of his body. The backed screen mentioned his parents, adding that she can summon a genie inside him to confirm to me what you are saying. And indeed for some time she gazed intently into the space in front of her, and after a moment some change in her consciousness should have occurred, her eyes began to arrange convulsive determination with incomprehensible words. When it is swallowed, asking, "Who are you?" And to my surprise, she replied to the screen, "I'm puzzled by the party. Use what the boy said to keep her from marrying someone who invites her to marry because he loves her, even though he insisted that her parents would kill her. Suddenly her movements revived and slowly returned to full consciousness, and when asked if you know what happened to her, she answered for.

He assured me of the parental engagement theme and, due to his daughter's illness, postponed the wedding many times. When I asked the family to leave me alone with my daughter for a few minutes after they left the room, I learned from the patient that she did not want to marry this guy, but from another one, except that his parents rejected him. She stated that sex affects them whenever you put in your marriage date.

Then it dawned on me that I was confronted with the turmoil of the breakup of my shift as a result of the pressure of parents in the marriage, because they do not enjoy the impedance transformation of the conflict within her into these attacks that lead to delay. Fortunately, the screen was not aware of these attacks, for which it was able to cause seizures on its own, having inserted a companion decision in the absence of the creation of the Republic.

You can explain this to your parents and explain to her that her illness was caused by a lack of interest in the proposal, that the person confirmed to them that the illness would go away when you confirm that it was not. In fact, he assured the parents that the daughter did not give them consent and promised not to visit her against her will.

After about a month had passed on the father's screen alone, it was announced that the disease had disappeared completely and the girl was in good health and they were offering her and him to marry someone else.

Such cases often occur in rural communities, especially those that depend on the gender ratio, because the patient believes in advance that the faith or magician of the revelation is in the absence of the same in order to do this, and soon makes the subconscious mind that the revelation leads the role the patient in the play is dramatic without realizing it.

Some spiritual healers may practice to identify with this situation in themselves or in brokerage fun with a debilitating civilization that they invoke to see some things invisible and related to the patient. It can also make a situation where the patient is willing to the patient's receptivity high in order to assume the patient's acceptance of power in his ability to remove sex from his body.

Obsessive- compulsive disorder "obsessive- compulsive disorder": Disease-related وساوسهاin the form of ideas or mental images or removal of duplicates and continuing to live with the patient from time to time. These obsessions are obsessive and stupid, or naive or disgusting, imposed on the patient's brain, who may try to ignore or suppress them, or neutralize them with other thoughts or actions to no avail, and he knows that it is a product of his mind, which is not imposed from outside. This whisper, which causes anxiety in the patient, strongly influences his life and affects his professional, political and social functions.

Often these whispers of a sexual nature or aggressive dirty and disgusting or ideas are formed by repetition of the act or returned, as ablution, or exaggerated in audit and learning and development. Or ideas to predict what terrible will happen to him or to someone dear to you to heighten the horror. Homelessness in religious matters or the divine is why these whispers of the patient were most hated.

Scientifically, these whispers are attributed to genetic and biological reasons, psychological, and the patient understands that this is a product of his brain and is imposed from the outside only in order to think about the religious and the majority of the public, that they touch or the demon's whisper occurs in the patient's blood, so that his heart says or may cause epileptiforms that cannot afford them.

They considered the " Freudian " neurotic anxiety as a struggle between the desires of the "play" of a sexual and aggressive nature, which do not feel each other, and the desires of the "ego" and "superego," which gravitate towards the ideals and reality of the other. The clearly expressed desires of the individual, consciously repressed in the unconscious, pose a threat to the integrity of the individual as incompatible with the norms of the community, religious, cultural and similar to the ethics of the individual.

The "ego" of a mature person can exploit the defense mechanisms of various, most importantly, "axial lines" in order to control these desires and thoughts, carefully think over interviews with them, hide them in the subconscious. But sometimes the process of repression is weakened by the fact that when it is foreseen by the conscious mind, then you reveal these desires or tendencies through your consciousness of the individual in the form of sexual and aggressive ideas, and not that the ego quickly restores the process of repression, again imagining these thoughts and desires animal from the consciousness of the individual. But I often find these thoughts and desires of an animal on the way to the surface, when the ego is weakest in daytime sleep or nighttime dreams.

A patient with schizophrenia is characterized by such conflicts of an unconscious or repressed nature that make him live in a state of preoccupation with a semi-continuous weakening of the repression process, therefore these tendencies and thoughts find their way out of the consciousness of the personality in the form
of paranoid or tendentious, or fantasies of sexual content, or aggressive, or doubts. and fears that constantly hurt or harass the individual and therefore try to resist or neutralize them or ignore them without success.

You may be asking a psychiatrist why these whispers are integrated in all parts of the world? And why stop the devil whispering this without reading the Koran on a sick non-Muslim ? How and why do I not answer that the devil is most often an extensible thing?

- D genetic diseases: "hereditary diseases"

Many of the genetic diseases that can be born in humans are associated with mental retardation or a significant decrease in IQ with congenital malformations of prominent parts of the body such as the skull, ears, eyes and hands. Or be silent or unconscious fish or a system that makes it scary house and
behaves stranno.Eti patients may believe that sex is inhabited by them, or whether they are from the people of sex .-------------- --------
--- -------------------

Scientific reasons for the appearance of oil:
You can define mental illness as an illness that causes impairment in thinking, perception, and emotion. In the case of being, the patient's capabilities are sharply limited in the face of the requirements of his professional and family life, social and even her

requirements, caring for the body and appearance, feeding himself or protecting himself from dangers.

In the most serious cases, patients may lose their understanding and quite a tendency to actually recognize right from wrong balance of extreme disorders in their contract, which reaches the stage of loss of reason or insanity specifically. When he lifted his pen and considers himself legally responsible for his actions, but does not stop him from taking action to prevent his oil or gas damage in the future, as booking him asylum speaks of his treatment and care.

Although the underlying cause of most physical and mental illness is not precisely known, medical research has confirmed that various factors, biological uses and the environment play an important role in the onset of this condition. Some of these disorders are associated with a deficiency or imbalance of chemicals in the brain called neurotransmitters . These connectors help brain cells communicate with each other, and any disruption of this balance in these conductors at hand, quantitatively and
qualitatively qualitatively, can result in no flow of messages or signals between cells in a normal way, leading to pathological symptoms.

Biological reasons:
1.heredity 2.inflammation 3 - damage to the brain before, during and after childbirth or lack of growth 4. insufficient nutrition 5 - exposure to toxins such as iron.

Reasons for selling:
1 - sexual abuse or difficult physical childhood. 2. denial or neglect of emotional or loss of mother. 3 - difficulties in belonging to others 4. constant feeling of inefficiency with low self-confidence is low.

Environmental reasons:

Includes housing, food, poverty, deprivation, as well as the use of alcohol, drugs, harmful work. As it is clear, there is no reason for the obvious one, but several factors are attributed together and when the almighty God, if the role of the devil in this is through or obsessive, but science does not support this. In addition to what was said above, I can say that I Throughout my studies and my rights to psychiatry, I did not go through a single condition that I suspected that they did not fall under the diagnostic criteria of psychiatry, and I also did not hear about the nature of myself as a person who is one of my own, as one who meets the army rather than mental illness. This does not negate the class of doctors, psychotherapists, psychologists and special psychics who, under hypnosis, turn to those who believe without sex or live in the events of what they are experiencing. And it gives knowledge that, in the absence of hypnagogic overtones, says that the sex or soul has left his body and, thus, he must suffer from its symptoms.

Not on the street, but on a cold evening, the four of us with my friends gathered around a small fire, the remaining fuel left palm leaves, the shadow of our large balcony overlooked the street. The air was heavy, saturated with moisture, the sky was covered with clouds, dense to blackness, since to improve them there were occasional short showers, accompanied by lightning and thunder. What were we doing on the street at this hour ... - I don't know. ... Capricious guys ... and more ... and the desire to smoke a cigarette out of sight of parents. At that time, more than two decades ago, there were no entertainment venues as diverse as they are today, there were no computers, no mobiles, no MBC space channels ! ... It is the street that is the most popular recreation area for most children and young people.

Among all the nights we spent on the sidewalk of the street, that night was suspended in my mind even to this day, not only because of the fact that she was cold, lonely and scared, but also because of the nature of the conversation that we explained at that meeting .. the conversation reflects a wide range of beliefs about sex and a haunted house.

* * *

- "Most of the haunted bathrooms are part" .. - he whispered to my friend Yasir and he has a left and a right. as if someone was watching him and his words.

- "Why in the bathroom ?!" I said funny, I don't understand why it is convenient to choose the floor in the bathroom of the restroom and your home.

"Because the name of God is not mentioned in the bathroom ... that's what my grandmother said," he answered Yasiru and lowered his voice with the air of a coward who did not miss his gaze. For my friend, on the one hand, this is the most ardent sex story, on the other hand, this is the fear and horror of most of us before this story! .... And you see him dressed in horror that tells stories of my inexhaustible, eternal grandmother.

- Yes it is. - said our friend, another, and his name was well-groomed, confirming the words of Yasser .. continuing to speak confidently .. - in every bathroom there is a Leprechaun , some are good, others are evil. "

"I don't believe it, do you have evidence of what you are saying?" - I said, agitated and very alarmed by this conversation, that I often have strange dreams and I am afraid to sleep alone in my room. As I would, if I could change the course of the conversation, but I didn't want to look like a frightened coward in front of my friends.

- "Yes, I have proof" .. a well-groomed answer in a tone colored with something like a challenge, then he continued .. -I will tell you a story that you witnessed, it happened many years ago, in one of the chapters. " cold winter, "when I woke my mother early, as usual, at morning prayer. My mother is a religious woman who, since childhood, strives for things to be different. It was under the slime that there is so much for the cleanliness of the house, since she was least likely to hear my mother's sound of gurgling water flowing into the bathroom, Fri calculated that one of my brothers had forgotten about the water opened after he was killed, and helped to enter the bathroom to close crane. But she froze in her place to open the light in the bathroom, an old woman stood inside, her hair was white feline, she was dressed in a white long dress, and she had a broom in her hand, and she was busy cleaning the bathroom with great care! ... And my mother is a great woman of faith and is afraid only of God, they cry to that old woman and ask her about the reason for their presence in our bathroom? ... The rejected head of the old man turned to her mother, and she felt how a brilliantly strange mother's run ran through her body so that her eyes met the eyes of the old man, while John's face was kind and encouraging, but her eyes were also terrible, and they more like a cat's eyes. and they were shimmery and strange ... ".

Here were minted well-groomed, as if signed by him words, and hiding the fact that fear and curiosity and the silence of the night around us were on our lips to such an extent that if you threw a needle between us, the reputation of the voice on Earth would be clear.!. It seems that this scene has ennobled our friend with well-groomed actions in his silence, as if he wants to torment us even more, shouted together with our friend Yasir, finally he swallows his saliva with difficulty: "what happened then? .. tell us?"

Oriental tales terrify .. pounds bathroom
An old man wearing a white dress in our bathroom! ..

Well-groomed a little in his own way, as if he is preparing to give a speech, already secretly longing for us to see the rest of the story, then he continued to say: "the old man told my mother in a pleasant tone: please tell your children not to pee in the bathroom, I lived here for many years, and I feel comfortable with you, because you are a woman of faith and pure, but the urine of your children in the bathroom painfully pushed me ... and what should the old dogs do even without the light protection of their own .. and when I opened my mother again the light turned out to be that the old man had completely disappeared! "Later that day, I asked my mother what would happen if one of us had to pee in the bathroom, and confessed to my younger brother that the water cycle was busy, so I had to pee in the shower. Since then, she has transferred my mom to an extremely clean and clean bathroom so as not to harm its inhabitants. "

"This is a really strange story!" "I said I was worried.

- No, it's not strange how you think that the old man is one of the good guys, and their presence in the pool house, and there you know the stories of the strangest a lot of this story, - said our friend, Zaki then go plaintively: "It also happened with my uncle, the poor and his family .. ".

- What about your uncle? ... Yasser asked curiously .

Zaki said , "a few years ago, rented house, old city center, I turn around to go there with my family. The product turned out to be bad, it was abandoned for a long time and in an oriental style .. any in the middle of a large courtyard surrounded by stone on each side and from the stairs to the second floor. The bathroom was shared with the water cycle and the bottom of the stairs. "

"This is a big mistake. You shouldn't install the shower on the side of the water cycle" ... he said, well dressed, interrupting her.

- "And what's wrong with that?" .. - I was surprised.

- "Because the water cycle is a place of impurity, and the bathroom is a place where people from their clothes .. and the meeting of impurity with nakedness attracts demons can call a demon."

"Nonsense," I said to him something out of the harshness of an acquaintance: "we have a bathroom, and the shared bathroom in our apartment did not accidentally touch the demon, and they will not grieve ... why are you making this up ?! ".

- I did not say that this will happen inevitably, I said that it can cause a demonic ... nor that the possibility of its increase in the case of a water cycle is associated with a campaign "... he answered well-groomed - something nervously hanging in the silence, heavy with a chunk of Yasser, finally saying, "let's get out of this table .. please, Zaki ... finish your uncle's story, please."

Zaki made a short pause, as if trying to remember the events, and then continued: "I did not stay long at the residence of my uncle and his family, in that house, until I began to come across very strange things .. my uncle with his wife and small children, they all slept in a large and wide room on the first floor, and one night I woke up, my uncle got scared by the sound of the door of the room, and it opened by itself and stopped steps in the courtyard .. ran out, thinking that the thief could beat Tsuru home, but he was surprised to leave the gap in the place is perfect! .. They searched the whole house .. there was no one there! It was strange, and the strangest thing is repeated in the following nights .. it gradually increased ... creating a conflict in the room on its own .. And the television works suddenly, without touching one ... many times they heard the sound of someone talking and laughing in a weak voice ... the sound came from the bathroom and the water cycle, and these things often happen in the late hours of the night ... ".

"I seek refuge with God, and that's why I hate the old house," she said to Yasir in a trembling voice, already with a pale face.

He continued, Zaki said, "The strangest thing is that my little cousin, who is a child of three and a half years ... she told her mother to see a stranger coming in and out of the protection hand of the bottom of the stairs, she said that his the body was naked ... presented in the form of its strange .. cheap .. like the legs of a goat, but the uncle did not believe the baby's statements and thought she was imagining such things. "

Oriental tales terrify ... pounds bathroom
His case with the goat ..

- "Oh, great!" .. Dude Yasir was terrified and his body suddenly rumbled to the sound of thunder, the strange thing is that we didn't laugh at him, as we usually do in such situations. In fact, at that moment we were no less terrible than we were in a panic.

Since Zaki was a consistent blow that he left for his interview in our souls, he said with an accent where he wandered a lot and enjoyed the artificial: "Do you want me to finish the story or not? Warning, the more terrifying."

How I wished he would shut up, silencing us with this horror, but the well-groomed one hastily said: "No, please finish the story, Zaki ."

Continuing with Zaki , he said, "After a while, something unexpected happened ... they started to return to the house every day at noon, it was not one of his habits that can leave work to return to the house at this hour of the day, and the irony is that he left home again before the children returned from school a little. I noticed an amazing change in my aunt's actions when I returned early, the deciphering of the paper became more pleasant, and I continue this course until then, until I see my uncle and his wife one day, for some reason she was the wife of a free, beautiful woman, and during a hand-to-hand fight, my aunt said: who is looking when you return in the evening, I do not believe that you are the same person who will be here at noon! I was surprised to be free, the most amazing thing to say is .. And I swear that he was not there that day and that he did not go to this area for another day before the expiration of his work in the evening .. swore his wife, who gives the opportunity to swear , what he had to return home every day at noon and leave before the children returned from school, and to her words, and to her little child .. he was supported by the girl's mother, said a cold big: yes, dad returned every day at noon, and then was naive: but made the door at noon. I don't like feet now, because feet are like goat's legs !! ".

- "Oh, that's very cute" .. dude Yasser again, this time as a cry plus if we are all taken from every outlet. There was silence for a moment, and then Zaki said:

"My uncle's wife, he almost fainted when I heard that she said her daughter was little, she swore that she would not stay in this terrible house for a minute. The truth is, my uncle also felt so intimidated by what was happening, despite his demonstrated solidarity and courage in front of his wife. But it was already enough that evening, and there was no longer in the arch the patience of the stripper, he gathered his uncle and wife some kind of bat carrying his clothes and left the house to hurry with his children, and was no longer free in the house terrible memory again only for furniture collection and purposes. "

"What a story," she said, well-groomed which gives us a closer look, and then continued, "I think the sex was impressed by your uncle's wife's love for her, they, as you say, a beautiful woman, deceived the same perception in your uncle's body .. lol cousin you never found him, never, and children can see things that we cannot see because they are innocent and pure. "

- "Jin loves people! ... It doesn't make sense," I said, I'm just stunned.

- Yes, it happens so often, my men in sex can admire human women ... and women in sex can love men from the United States, "said well-groomed and supported Yasser said:

- "That's right, something like that happened near my university ... at that moment I was taking a shower in the bathroom, and she was standing in the shower blindfolded, when suddenly she felt a strange feeling and an irresistible desire to open her eyes .. he opened her and found that her elf was ugly with a huge head, his face was dark and scary, and his eyes were red, as if they were

turning into fire, and from shock he passed out on my cousin, who
was in place, and when the dwarf regained consciousness, he
disappeared , and then her parents began to notice some changes
in her behavior .. now many lost people do not speak too much ..
And turn it on strongly when you hear the reading of the Koran,
and more than once in the same day .. And complained to her
parents about the fact that they are infected with demonic,
introduced her to one of the dates, confirmed his doubts, told them
that the kilograms had already fallen in love with their daughter
and her body, and were not able to get the thing out of sex, but
diligently, and then the girl returned to her doctor first. "

Oriental tales terrify .. pounds bathroom
His eyes were red as if they had set off two lights ..

"Already there are a lot of such things, both with women and men
.. and this story is similar to what happened to one of my relatives,"
he said to Zaki , ready to retell the facts of the new story, but I
interrupted him with a shout :

- "Enough, enough ... when I don't want to hear anything else," I
told her nervously, and then you meet with my friends, without
even saying goodbye, and promise me to go home, and I'm
ashamed to shake to shake, and not hide that I could not sleep well
that night, and the necessary fear for several nights, so I cannot be
alone in my room, and when alienated most of the campaign, so
beware. my parents so, they insisted on taking a shower, so as not
to harm the surrounding smell of my body, killing by force, and as
soon as I could, but I really wanted not to close my eyes for a
minute and blink eyelids even when you feel free soap .. after these
tales I've heard .. who knows what awaits me in the bathroom ?!

* Note from the author: I have not seen kilograms in my life, and I
have a desire to see someone, and I do not know exactly how
strong my health is and the fact that anecdotes are presented in

this story, I have already heard from some of my friends who claimed that this is real .. and you have the choice to believe or discredit this story is entirely up to you, dear reader.

Mysterious .. rain man

There are people all over the world, of different religions and cultures - some believe in the demonic, others are no longer your only form of cruel illusion father registrar means a dirty mark on simpletons who believe that all cases of what is called a demon are in fact her mental illness with an impact on the character and behavior of the source, for example, changing the tone of his voice and speaking in good faith with someone else, or reporting actions not together, like beating his family members and those close to him for no reason ..

But if some things, such as changing sound and behavior, are understandable and reproducible. what is the interpretation of doing things supernatural, for example, adjusting to a language that I do not know, you move things from a distance. flying in the air ..

Or remove the rain from the ceiling of the room ?! ... Just like the hero of our story ..

Skeptics will say that most of what they see around those obsessed with the deeds of the supernatural, in fact, her stories are not documented, not confirmed ..

But the story (Don Decker) differs from the rest of the story in the presence of many witnesses who confirmed their appearance, some of them from the police and law enforcement agencies.
But hey .. who is Don Decker ? ..
Don or Donnie , as his friends call them, is a person who was born in the US state of Pennsylvania. He lived his childhood, was tormented, tormented, and ended up being sent to prison to serve a sentence for one year after the fastest shop.

In 1983, when he was twenty-one, I got Donnie a week off from prison to attend his grandfather's funeral. In fact, Donnie was not sad about his grandfather, on the contrary, he felt great comfort from the departure of the stern old man, while it caused him mental and physical pain, since he was a child of about seven years, a secret that he did not know many people.

Donnie came to his hometown and attended his grandfather's funeral, stood by the body of an old man lying motionless in a wooden coffin before he was buried, meeting his bitter memories and feelings mixed between pain and sadness, anger and gloating, also remembering how he wounded his this old man, and how he left a scar that will not erase on his soul.

After the funeral, he wanted Donnie to go to the building in his house, but his mother refused to enter his house, she was bitter about it because he went to jail. And that's why his wife Jenny was able to guess the guest at the house of his old friend Bob.
In the evening, he ushered Donnie into an adjoining guest bathroom on the top floor of his friend's house, he wanted to wash his hands before he went down to dinner with Bob and Jenny. And while he was soaping his hands, I suddenly felt a strange feeling, as if the air had been completely removed from the library, and rushed through his body so coldly, and then there was a strange feeling that someone was watching him, raised his head and looked in the mirror in front of him over the sink, he saw in him the

reflection of the pale face of an old man, similar to his grandfather, the old man was seen in a strange way and on his face was an evil yellow smile.
It seemed to Donny that the old man who was standing behind him quickly looked around his face, but there was no one there, and then he returns to the sink, with horror, sees how red scars appeared on his hands, does not know where they came from, how as if someone had put their nails into his wrists.

Then suddenly it all stopped as soon as he began, usually airy, to talk about the nature of his faded old man's face, but the scars were still visible on my wrist without me, and later, when he went down to the dinner table, he asked his friend Bob about these scarred, Donnie said that it appeared on his wrists all of a sudden and that he thought something was wrong in the bathroom upstairs, but Bob replied with a laugh that it was just a fantasy.

After dinner, relax Donnie and Bob and Jenny in the living room for coffee, while they talk, I feel like Donnie again the cold that gripped his body in the bathroom, and then she screamed Jenny suddenly she gestured towards the wall, he looked at everyone there where she pointed, there were drops of water running down the walls, and then began to crumble heavily from the ceiling. The house was strange and confusing, it was raining in the living room! ..

Bob began to carefully examine the walls, and then went upstairs, it seemed to him that one of the water pipes was probably broken, but to his great surprise everything was normal and dry in the whole house except the living room. And since Bob was hired for this, I called the owner of the original house and asked him to come urgently.

It took only a few minutes even Ron , the owner of the original house, who lived in a neighboring house on the same street, was even present , and he brought his wife with him, and soon had an amazing Monday language and they watched what was happening in the living room, because they were familiar with all the secrets of the house the following Monday, tirelessly checking all pipes, tanks and connections, but finding no fault, everything seemed to sound in his store ..

So where is the money ?! ...

Mysterious. ... Rain Man
So where is the money? ..

It is exactly the same question that his face is a bob for two John Boogie and Richard Wolpert they entered their house after the oriental determine what was going on. And just like it happened with Ron and his wife, the police at first thought that it had something to do with the bursting water pipe, but when they checked the walls, the incredible happened, she no longer just fell from the roof, but began to jump horizontally from one wall to the other and dangle upside down from floor to ceiling! ...

The policemen were shocked and horrified, they had never seen anything like it in their lives.

Then suddenly Jenny screamed: "Oh, look at Donnie !" ..

He gave the beauty to Donny , which they completely forgot about in the midst of their worries and searches for the source of the mysterious. Donnie was still sitting in his place in the corner of the room, holding a cup of coffee in his hand, he was motionless and motionless like a statue, his face was very pale, and there was a blank look in his eyes, as if he was floating in another world and living something that was happening around him.

The officers advised Bob and Jenny to get out of Donnie because he looks very sick, they asked them to go and wait at the pizzeria for the return of the product until the company decided exactly what was going on in the region.

The most amazing thing is that once he left Donnie with Bob and his wife until the rain stopped in the living room. beware of him only that once all three sat down in the pizzeria restaurant, before the rain began to crumble over their heads, this time inside the restaurant! ...

The Old Man's author saw what was happening and looked closely at Donnie , he didn't like her, he whispered in Jenny's ear that she believed Donnie might know the Demon and asked them to leave the restaurant immediately. naturally surprised everyone that there were three left until the rain stopped inside the restaurant.

While Bob and his wife, while the bailiffs were at the house, left, saying that they would bring more support to achieve this. The three of them sat down in the kitchen, and Jen began to organize the pale Preble in front of Donnie's face with great clear horror. Then again strange things began to raise their heads, this time starting the pots and plates to vibrate violently by themselves, in fact everything in the kitchen was being taken care of as if it were an earthquake. Jenny lost her mind, so he angrily yelled at Donnie and accused him of being the cause of all these strange things that suddenly hit her house. But Donnie did not answer, he seemed still not aware of what was happening around him, but he got up from his seat, suddenly stopped near the table motionless, then Jenny's startlingly loud screams rose a little into the air, and then broke off and fell on the wall, as if someone had thrown her away, and when he got up from his seat, it looked like I had just woken up again, that empty expression on his face faded and calmed the house, I stopped all strange and mysterious.

However, the lull did not last long, the next day the city police visited the house of Bob and Jenny, so as not to tell the cops about the mysterious, did not believe them so much that he wanted to see for himself how he examines the product, the return of the repression of strange inferiority, the rigidity almost on the spot suddenly appeared , and a light fog quickly, so that the cloud was white over the stairs to the upper floor towards the lobby, caused amazement and amazement, everyone began to rumble in a mosaic of clouds, and then pouring rain fell over the head of the city police and his companions, the man ran away from the house and he disappeared. does not twist on something, saying that these special cases are not within the competence of the police and that they can do nothing to help.

When I left Mae's anger company just bullying my pocket, I was about to ask Donnie to leave her house, but Bob and I object to it because of the friendship that binds him without it, luckily for the couple, then Donnie's vacation is over and he was on my way back to my prison.

Donnie returned to his cell, he still did not understand after what happened over the weekend, sat contemplating the miracle that was happening, which I noticed at that moment when I saw the old man's face in the bathroom mirror, and then suddenly an idea lit up in his head that surprised with the same ... Oh, can you see what you can do to make the rain fall inside the cell? ..

Mysterious. ... Rain Man
I took it to rain inside the chamber ..

Their amazement returned to the same hazy light that he had seen in Bob's house, and then water droplets began to drip , bouncing wildly over the walls, ceiling and floor ... it was raining in the cell! ..

Prison guards watched what was happening
inside Donnie's dungeon and he did it on purpose, spraying the walls and ceiling with toilet water and threatening to punish

him. But Donnie denied that he had to spray the walls with water, he told the guards that he for some mysterious reason does not know himself, then he can make it rain anywhere at any time. The guards, of course, did not believe his words, they asked him to prove it by making it rain over the head of a prisoner in a nearby cell. Indeed, a few moments later a mysterious cloud appeared in the next cell, and then it began to fall on the head of another prisoner, who almost fainted from horror.

The daze Rahu guards are carefully examining the walls of Donnie's cells adjacent to them, they thought that this was a kind of trick, and for a guarantee, they asked me to make it so that the rain fell over the head of the security officer, who is in his office at the end of the corridor, which lined with cameras on either side of it. Naturally, not even a minute passed for the general amazement when the officer left his room and froth himself, and the students from the guard began to look for the cause of the water flowing from the walls and ceiling of their room.

The guards told the officer the truth about what was going on and about Donnie Huck 's ability to shoot rain .. they were even called Rain Man (Rain Man He said that the patrol officer in turn would pass this story on to the director of the prison, said that this was Donnie's last visit and inspection on your own, verify that his abilities, but he noted with suspicion that the change was suppressed by Donnie's face when you care to send rain, and if he is fully convinced that he possessed, which is why I turned to the adjacent church to the prison, and asked them to send a priest to conduct a ritual to expel evil spirits from Donnie's body . Indeed, the pastor was present and brought Donnie into the cell until he blinded a new eye with a mysterious fog. But the pastor was not frightened, I had seen similar things before In novels about how long the weather took, some say that it lasted several hours and saw horrific things happening, while others They say it only took a few minutes, no matter how long it took Donnie to finally get rid of the evil that greeted his body, hasn't addressed this situation since.

The Case Without Dick Think of more cases of demonic glory obsession, this is a unique case, not only strange events, but there are many witnesses who have confirmed their reliability. The story is in several television programs, the most famous
being Paranormal Witness in the first season of 2011.

Rushdie building in Alexandria

A building of enormous color melancholy freezes when time, as if enveloped in deep sleep, for a long time and dully turns to everything that surrounds it, from the bustle of Bruit and the hustle and bustle. And taking care also of the big screen that has been around for many years, they are known to all the inhabitants of Alexandria, especially the residents of the Rushdie district , produced on the side of one of the abandoned streets, which is becoming throughout the many myths that it is said to have left long ago. long ago due to what was happening with things, things strange things are not planned on PayPal and can only be seen in horror movies. What happened after all? ..

Accidents, terrible, dear reader, tragic things made the inhabitants of that ill-fated game black day that I stepped into the territory of the damned ..

There are many stories told by people, some talk about a man who jumped off the top floor for some unknown reason, and it was frankly scary that only the silence of the night is the last thing he left behind, and there is also that Greek guy who drowned him and his entire family in a fishing boat accident after just two days of his stay with words, and there is also a story about a bride who saw blood flowing from the walls of his apartment and then his black cat is big! ..

Strange and mysterious events continued to stand inside the action until the closed guard opened their doors to the back and stones and left them so angry ... and since then it has become so that people in Alexandria talk, just looking at him , and run in front of him so as not to catch up with them in terms of basis.

But what is the reason for the curse that befell the steam? ...

Some legends claim that the work was under construction when it fell to the Quran from one client and was built to work on it .. you say that the Land of Architecture was built over a mosque that was torn down by a contractor who built a working machine .. there are also those who say that the architecture was built over the cemetery, and some are buried in those who died in tragic mysterious incidents, therefore inhabited by goblins who work behind their backs scare anyone who dares to approach her dwelling. Another story claims that there are contractors involved in the construction of architecture, but one of them really cheated the other and gave him his money, and the last spell work (work) has one of the magic of two black magic, he pushed the spell into the foundations of the building to get to one.

Fairy tales

The story or Legend of the most sought-after building is that it was built in 1961 and was owned by a man who brought his family to live with it, but it was only a few days in his residence at work until he died and sons after he sank his boat while fishing, and after the death of " Khawaji " sold his wife's working car and left the country.

The employer of the new car decided to rent out his apartments, but jinxed everyone who tried to live in them, the guy who rented the first floor died as a result of a powerful fire that broke out in his apartment after a short period of his residence in it, the doctor who rented the second floor, died in a car accident a few days after the opening of his clinic. In the second round, I hired a woman who lives alone because her children are working abroad and a few days later they found him dead and did not know to never be judged. There, a trading company rented the fourth floor, but soon it went bankrupt and the owner died on a permanent basis.

Over the course of several months of the story, they tell the story of her to the villain's fiancée, who paid for the housing crisis in order to secure the strong company that dominated the control action to rent one of the apartments. that happens. the beginning of the nineties of the last century, say, that first night so poor in architecture of the bride was Red Noisy Night, not because it is a night of income, but because of something that happened somewhere beyond imagination ..
That night, the crowd saw a stain of blood on the walls of the groom and his bride, and then they began to taps and pour blood-red water, and he seemed to them like a black giant cat, And when he tried to run away from the cat, they found a headless woman, waiting for them in the living room, and her severed head lying on the floor, laughing loudly in alarm ... The Arab man got scared and ran to the door of the apartment, and found that the door had disappeared, and there was a terrible black man at home with long and sharp fangs waiting for them, he opened his mouth to cool

them and did not feel a thing after that, and found that two people passed out on the street half naked the next morning.

It is estimated that each of the residential buildings has architecture after its furniture was found smashed and thrown into the street in the morning! .. and that the orcs shook the building so that its inhabitants and blood flowed from the taps .. and doors and windows opened and closed on their own ..

And when they came to the imam to read the training and the goblin theme ... and the staircase architecture disappeared! Yes, dear reader, I did not find a single thing handed over to him and when he tried to enter the apartment on the ground floor, you chose the doors of the apartments !! .. And that after a period in which the Sheikh was present, the latter ridiculed the tales of people from the orcs inhabiting architecture .. and decided to stop alone at work in order to prove to people that everything that happens around her fairy tales is just an unfounded myth .. and in fact In fact, the first day passed peacefully without any incident, the second too .. and the third .. the fourth .. so people thought that what was installed and that all this about architecture was just nonsense, but this conclusion did not last long .. The day before I woke people up to leave the thing lying on the street and its furniture around him, broken and scattered on the ground, and when they asked him who did this to him, he could not answer the severity of the horror, says that he died a few days later from the severity of the shock.

Proposed architecture
Far from what other residents of the surrounding area say about architecture, the ancients say that all the myths about architecture are unfounded , and that the reason, which is free of the population even to this day, is that the owner died after the completion of the rebuilt soon felt his heirs about her and remained abandoned until now because of this disagreement.

This story is confirmed by a group of young people who worked in 2012 at the invitation of a person by someone on Facebook , there are photos and videos on the network showing how these young people waving their hands from the balconies of the action after they entered it through the parking lot. nearby, challenge some of these guys, burst inside, saying that they have not seen anything strange or supernatural habit in the interior, as well as the architecture of the unfinished construction, where the walls are not yet sheathed with plaster, which indicates that no one has lived in to this car, therefore, all the stories that have been told about the building are unfounded .

But regardless of the storming of the building, many people still believe that the big secret was discovered by this architecture, if there is a dispute between the heirs it actually makes sense to continue from the sixties until now! .. and from the logical left, how this huge estate is worth millions up to the polite in this picture .. well, who pays the salary to the boss and his family? ... And that they blocked the architectural brick door. why all this mystery and secrecy, and unless those people who come to work by car at night in modern cars and leave before morning, as some residents of the region claim ... is there really something happening inside this building and the prosecution is trying to hide it and cover with tales of goblin or ghosts? ... All these questions remain unanswered.

Glimpses of the jinn world

We have all, no doubt, heard and read enough about them to satisfy our curiosity. But our dear readers, in these lines of the expected range, we will be exploring things that were not on the account of this hidden world .. are you ready? .- Is your heart strong enough? - Can you continue? If you supplement this article with me, you are strong in heart, and if not, then I advise you not to go there.

Let's start ...

A few months ago I was told by some friends a story about a wizard Rouhani in one of the Arab states, this processor is an old cent reader in that he is an expert in cancer treatment and the like.

This processor has a wonderful history, one night, I went to see him a woman, hearing about him as a Rebel in the treatment of some incurable diseases by doctors.
This woman gave birth to her daughter at the age of 16 in the interest of, I noticed that several signs proved beyond any doubt that he was obsessed with sex. Already one of the relatives used this woman after I told him that she was going to this therapist due to the fact that her son's condition became critical, and with hundreds of miles until they reached the praise of God to the processor, and the son's diagnosis , and found that he was already possessed, asked the processor of the mother and her relatives to be a little, until he read some verses of the Koran to get out of this body sex.

During the first session, the therapist reads something, of course, plus the restraining order, which is to force sex at the checkout otherwise it would not have happened.

The genie was very clever when he read aloud and then came back! ....

And to my amazement, the mother and her relatives get from this something in suspicion in their hearts, the ability of this processor .. or the birth of a normal one .. and Tara says with a genie .. sometimes they beat the same way !! ..

He told them to the wizard that this was the strangest case of two in his life, which are about five years old in this task.

During the second session, the more the Wizard of Containment, and the more read in the startling so began the birth of nausea and much to strike terror in the hearts of those present. Then tell them the processor that he ended up giving Mom a sigh of relief.

Surprise..

Tell the sorcerer the people of the state that we need to try it so don't come back at all, that's what happened between them, from their edges ...

The question is: why did he enter his body? ...

Genie: Because he once hurt me and poured hot water.
Sheikh: Don't you know it's unfair? ...

Genie: ... not responding ...

Sheikh: Tell me a little about the jinn.

Genie: We are just like you humans in everything we eat, drink, sleep, are born and die.

Sheikh: It is rumored that you always have red eyes .. Is it true? ...

Genie : Not always .. but it's not round like human eyes, but oval.

Sheikh: Describe me in more detail.

Genie: Our ears are like the ear of a horse, and our noses are in the middle of the face like humans. Women have a lot of hair, but little in men who have a lot of baldness.

Sheikh: And your legs and arms? ...

Genie: Our hands are the same as yours, except that they vary in length: they are longer compared to our body, and our nails are long, and our feet are flat and pointed.

Sheikh: What are your colors? ...

Genie : Various .. but most of them are black.

Sheikh: Satan is the father of the jinn? ...

Genie: Iblis is not one of the genies, and he is not their father.

Sheikh: Then what is the name of Abu al- Jana ? ...

Genie: His name is Poison.

Sheikh: What is the difference between a genie and a devil? ...

Genie: Satan is a genie, not every genie is a demon.

Sheikh: How old are you? ...

Genie : 180 years old, you're still young !! ...

Sheikh: Tell me about the genies in general.
El Jinn: Our life system is complex, as each tribe is ruled by a
king. We do not have a shura system , but the government rules,
and our tribes have many.

Sheikh: How are jinn prepared? Tell us more about me.

Genie: Azazir is visiting the bathroom, and this person must be
unclean .. Olives, and he is visiting the bathroom in the form of a
black cat .. Sarukh must be (naked) and recite the determination to
be present .. Danhash wakes up you in the form of a man in a
turban ..

As for the daughters of the devil .. the same beauties bring to you
after reading the definition in the cemeteries .. with his eye the
magician writes talismans in his hand and then he sleeps, and you
come up to him and wake him .. daughters of daughters come to
your bathroom and ask marry one of them .. favorably The
Magician reads talismans and spells and sleeps without the purity
of his girlfriend And wakes him up ..

Nassour is the genie most mages fear. The doorman's son squirrel
comes to the bathroom and has talismans and intentions that the
wizard says.

Sheikh: What are you making up? ...

Genie : We are formed in all forms ... But our favorite forms are
cats, dogs and snakes.

Sheikh: You are types, right? ...

Genie: Yes.

Sheikh: Who are you afraid of genies? ...

Genie : Genie because he's so aggressive.

Sheikh: What are you? ...

Genie: I am a resident of the house (Amer).

Sheikh: Do you have courts and a judge? ...

Genie: Yes, just like you.

Sheikh: Where do jinn often live?
Genie : We love mountains very much, especially high mountains and seas, especially oceans and islands.

Sheikh: If the genie is represented by a human, how can I tell him apart if I don't know? ...

Genie: He has two things ... Firstly, his eyes are oval, not round like humans. And it would be very warm myself.

Sheikh: Are his legs really like those of a donkey? ...

Genie: No, not always.

Sheikh: Jinn have two horns, as we heard? ...

Genie: Yes, but their size varies from genie to genie.

Sheikh: What tribe are you from? ...

Al-Jin: From the orders ... of the heads of the houses.

Sheikh: Can you fly? ...

Genie: No, it is common for some genies, and they cannot fly at all.

Sheikh: That is, genies cannot fly, but this is just property.
Genie: There is a type called flying genies that are isolated from genies because they often fly in the air, but most genies do not fly, but rather look like you.

Sheikh: What's your name? ...

Genie: Mustafa.

Sheikh: Do you mean that you are a Muslim? ...

Genie: Yes.

Sheikh: Do you repent or not? ...

Genie: I swear to God I'll never come back.

Sheikh: Do you swear to God? ...

Genie: Yes.

Sheikh: Go away, God help you.

The boy returned safely to his home after this genie tortured him, and his mother was very happy and sacrificed her dignity for him and prepared a feast for this, and everyone was happy with the boy's return to school after he was absent all the time. during which he was absent. was obsessed. He grew up and is now working as a manager for a large company in an Arab country.

From the words of the genie we conclude that the genies are present, but with certain talismans, and that the genies are bodies and bodies, not spirits, as some claim, and that the genies eat, drink, are born and die, and that the genies are many tribes. and that the jinn are often in the form of cats, snakes and dogs and are often black, and that the jinn in their reality are replete with dark skin, and that their true forms are not terrible as we imagine, but they are strange, and that their age is very great in comparison with people, and we put them in danger at any moment, but it has signs, and that genies cannot fly, as we thought, but this is a characteristic that some of them have, and that we can distinguish between genies if they are formed in the form of a man, and that the jinn have what is called construction, and they are with us in our houses, and we do not see them, and that the jinn in them are good and bad, and we must beware of them and not pour hot water into the empty place or bathroom, for example, we must be careful because they are present in the Doves, as we are. know and that they prefer to live in higher elevations, not in the way we previously thought that they are underground or that they prefer to live in arid lands such as deserts or the like, and that they also inhabit seas, especially oceans and islands, and they will not harm us if We have caused them direct pain.
Mating genies and humans
Glimpses of the jinn world
The marriage of jinn and humanity worries many.

Mixed marriages of genies with humans have been the concern of many people for centuries because it is a unique condition ... But is it really possible? ...

We will first touch on a few things, the first of which is how to do it? ..

Then let's see how the meeting of the spouses, what to do?

Finally, we will mention excerpts from some books on this matter.

Marriage is a meeting of spouses, man and woman, and one of its most important goals is to preserve gender for us as humans, and this is one of the laws of life since God created our father Adam and until life ceases to exist. exist on the face of the world ... And it entered the Holy Quran: (O people, we created you from a man and a woman, and we made you peoples and tribes so that they know each other.)

Now we come to the question of mating with genies.

Several months ago I was in the market and I was shopping at the time and my friend was with me. We went into one of the perfume shops (a shop that sells vapors and perfumes) and we needed oud and it is well known ... Long before that I had heard of something called men's chewing gum, which is also a type of vapor and I suddenly remembered this, so I told the seller about this incense and asked him if it exists? ..

His answer was very strange, so he told me that he exists, but it is forbidden! ..

I told him: So how do you sell it? ..

He told me that there are certain buyers who come to buy it, but other people don't! ..

Did I tell him why? ..

He said literally: this incense is associated with jinn.

I was surprised by this problem and we left Al- Attar and I talked to my friend while I was between faith and lies. A few days later, I called one of my friends when he was abroad and he was known among us at a young age for his imaginative powers ... The important thing was that I called him and told him to give me a name book, dedicated to the science of spirituality, so he told me that it would be easy for you with this book and told me his name.

Indeed, it was with great difficulty that I acquired the book, knowing that it was not on the Internet.

And the main purpose of the whole book was to download the genies. The book was really terrifying and very old, when you grabbed it you would feel a shudder ... but I strengthened my heart and read it, and gradually I learned what I did not know before ..

Important note "What I am about to post is very dangerous and it is from a text book ..

Preparing a beauty queen for marriage
Glimpses of the jinn world
Miss Genie ..

This queen rules over 3700 kings, and each king rules over 700 tribes, the number of which only God knows.

Working method

Two times later, you accept spiritual permission ... (This paragraph has been deleted by the site administration) .. On the eighth night, you see a light filling the space, so don't be afraid. On the ninth night, you see black cats and eggs .. Don't be afraid. On the tenth night, you see many moonlike women and they tell you, "Take one of us and leave this job." Then tell them that I want a beauty queen and they will leave you. On the eleventh night, women will come to you like the moon, and in the middle of them there will be a beauty queen, like the sun, with priceless clothes and ornaments, and behind them the judge, and they will greet you, peace be upon you This paragraph is made by the site's management).

The use of Afra bint Afar
This is for love, answer quickly ... (This paragraph has been deleted by the site management).

....

These are excerpts from a book whose title (............) This is a very dangerous book and reference for the ancient magicians.

How to get married
The specialist tells me who is knowledgeable, not a magician ... that marriage with genies is common, it is very easy and does not require the impulse found in the books from talismans, wakefulness, retreats , etc.

I also asked him about how a genie or genie appears, and he told me that it will appear to you the way you want it, but that has a condition ...

I told him what is it? ..

Jin told me that once you get married, you must not marry someone, forget him, otherwise woe to you! ..

He told me an old story, the content of which is that there is a man with disabilities, so whenever he offers to propose to one of the girls, he is rejected, so what of him, except that he went to one of the magicians and asked him to marry a pound, so the magician agreed, and the wedding ceremony really took place, and among the conditions mentioned above was the condition: the man lived with his magic wife, and she came to him with a picture of a brown but charming girl.

He was at his workplace for several days, and he liked his girlfriend at work because of his calmness, so she openly asked him to marry him, so he agreed and forgot about the contract between him and his fairy wife. On the same day, he made the girl an offer to make the girl, they found him killed, and there were traces of scratches on his face !! ...

I was very shocked when he said and I was surprised ... This is just one of thousands of stories and you can believe or deny ..

The genie takes revenge on everyone who sees him!

For many years she was a sad and familiar companion to the life of the Richard family in their huge house, built in the middle of the nineteenth century. Many family members, old and young, ended their lives in madness or died mysteriously and for no apparent reason. Some of them were found dead in his bed with their mouths open. you know, there are signs of panic on his face, as if he saw something terrible just before his death. Others committed suicide by shooting over their heads, some jumped out of the windows of the upper platform, hanged themselves there and disappeared without a trace ... the strangest thing is that all these people were healthy and did not suffer from any diseases or mental disorders.

Photo of kilograms of everyone who sees it!
Shadows of the evil eye and companions of the hearth.

The bottom line is that Richard's family nearly died out during the eight contracts that ruled this ill-fated home, another member of the madman's family contributed mental health. The port left home life, it became abandoned only from darkness and silence, and soon rumors circulated in its language, it was said that ghosts were following it, and that a demon from another world was coming to the gate.

But Mr. Johnson, a successful banker, you do not need any of these stories, he is a rational person, not superstitious, he does not miss investment opportunities found in the region, because so many turned away from buying him because of his reputation, creepy, and that is why low lot price.

Mr. Johnson bought and rebuilt the house and then moved in with his family. He didn't ask the lender until strange things began to peek out of the corners of the old house and ... the doors open and close on their own, the targets of moving the dishes are intact, the sounds and screams of anonymous people resonate throughout the region. Mr. Johnson's daughter began to suffer a little from strange symptoms, stopped buying food, turned pale in face, and until the end she was pursued by insomnia and anxiety, and persuaded her father to see something wrong in her, she told him that she sobbed, as she woke up from time to time to see a huge black a cat sitting on the edge of her bed, which, in tune, filled them with hatred, and sometimes showed a terrible person dragging her by the hair.

He didn't believe Mr. Johnson that what was happening in the region had something to do with another, but at the same time he had no explanation for the things of others that don't spend every day. Finally, at the insistence of his wife, he moved his family to another place, he insisted on staying, he wanted to know the secret of what was happening. I advised my friend on the committee to a psychic. the famous formerly lived on the outskirts of town and Lady Elizabeth Port. But Mr. Johnson rejected this advice, snapping angrily that he would never resort to lawful and sorcerers, but he soon opposed his opinion a few days later. One dark night I wake up from a dream and see that his huge black cat is sitting on the edge of the bed and looking at him with shining eyes with two displays of malice.

Photo of kilograms of everyone who sees it!
The look fills them with hate ..

Mr. Johnson jumped out of bed in horror and a light came on from behind, looking for the cat, but he disappeared, searching the room again and again, but there was no sign of the cat.

But how did you get it? .. The door and windows were tightly locked .. where did he come from? ...

The shocks of that night did not fulfill Mr. Johnson's fantasies, especially those that looked foul and spiteful. Remember your daughter's words about a cat and a scary person, were her words true? The mere thought of this made his heart beat wildly, and in the end he decided to accept the advice of his friends and fans of the psychic.

On the same rainy night and stormy winter of 1933, the car stopped a black old-fashioned Ford in front of Richard's house and caught their middle-aged lady, dressed in a dark and continuing a black hat with a flowing openwork scarf covering the upper half of her face. Mr. Johnson took his guest at the party with a big stride and put him in his home, where three of Mr. Johnson's friends, a close friend who had decided to stay with him through a seance that was to take place at the house that night, were waiting for them.

Before Mr. Johnson about the nature of the terrible and mysterious things that happen in his house categorically by his store signs and the panic evident on her face, she whispered that she could feel the presence of an evil force, rudely controlled in the place where she is strongly present among them now. Then I asked the audience to lower their voices and brightness, and when they finished that, I made them all on a board around a large round table and Miss Johnson got the same thing in the air as symbols, signs, mysterious, and suddenly the rigidity of almost her body, with using her eyes, I measured her features, the table began shaking violently from under everyone's arms, and then a thin thread of smoke appeared, the center of the table behind the spreads slowly moved towards what looks like a cloud of small ones, taking the form of a man with the terrible features of four legs, like cats! ...

Photo of kilograms of everyone who sees it!
White smoke behind ..

One of Mr. Johnson's friends was a journalist, and he brought a camera with him and hid it in his bag without the knowledge of everyone, and while everyone was stunned and busy watching what was happening in front of them, from this press machine they shot an image of lightning at a speed up, so that the ethereal object posed terribly over the table, and for this they even shook the walls of the house violently, with the help of pillars, and then they heard a voice, as if rumbling like thunder, saying: "I will avenge you, I will avenge you." from the smoke and Mrs. Port fell unconscious.

When Mrs. woke up from a kind of coma, she was very angry, she said that there were other covenants and the Charter between her and the objects of the world, and that they were violated today, when a friend of Mr. Johnson took this photo during a meeting without knowing it, and only God knows what these objects would do if they were angry with them.

At the request of Mr. Johnson, my friend, a journalist who spoiled the image, I promised him to do it, but he did not keep his promise, the next morning the address of the wide top of the first page of the largest newspaper in the country appeared with the following content: "the first photograph of a real harvest in the world", and in this heading a creepy photo popped up with a detailed description of the facts of the seance held in the house, or rather.

It was not long before the decision of the terrible revenge of everyone who was present at that meeting ..

Miss Stor's body was found in the woods near her home, her limbs were amputated, her head extended, and her eyes got two marble ones next to her bloody body.

The journalist who took this photo died after a fire in his apartment.

Mr. Johnson found a product inside the pigeon, and its arteries were severed.

Two friends were two others who attended the meeting were crazy and mental health ideas.

The house is most likely the same one that was put up for burning a fluffy after a few months, turned into a heap of ash, nothing remained, which shows that you have nothing, not even a single image, as if it did not belong to this place once ...

Finally, what else is there to say? ... Praise the Lord that all the heroes of our story who died were killed or wounded all over the left edge. in the end, only the image is terrible, but about Syracuse, dear reader, I advise you not to prolong what you see.

Erk Hospital Mystery

You may be wondering what now ?! .. (Hospital of his race) .. stupid .. I've never heard of this before ... so tired of this shit, but enough to fabricate a lie ...

But wait, dear reader .. is it possible that you have not heard about this, and you are flipping through the pages of horror and surprise sites ..

Well, no problem, we will take you with us on a short trip to remember from this abandoned hospital not to reveal the subtleties and secrets that surround them from all sides .. we will contact you about horror stories, many of which related to tongue-tied, some incredible and some are talking the full width of the wall, but regardless of the truth, he turned this hospital into a landmark in Arab horror literature that has become controversial in Saudi society ..

Come with us, dear reader, dive into the depths of darkness, and reveal its secrets were his.

What is this hospital story?
Whatever one may say about the hospital, its history is that of an abandoned hospital currently located in the city of Riyadh, its construction was completed in 1987 by former Lebanese Prime Minister Rafik Hariri to donate it to the Kingdom's Ministry of Health Saudi Arabia . Of course, this novel was not confirmed there, although an official of the Saudi Ministry of Health points out about

the hospital: "it was created several years ago as a private one, but it did not work in a timely manner."

Regardless of which hospital is built, it seems at first glance similar to luxury and when you enter, you will be amazed by the impressive decor, and the space by a large and luxurious huge building ...

The hospital consists of eight floors and is fully integrated with all the appliances, elevators, lighting and electricity that are still available in the hospital.

And this begs a good question .. if the building is integrated and ready to go, why do you remain abandoned all these years? ... The answer is simply that the owner did not record the donation amount to the Ministry of Health of the Kingdom of Saudi Arabia before his death, real estate development from the building if they did not give the land price and construction costs, especially after seeing the area in which the hospital expanded with a thriving urban rise in value land that belongs above. Over the years, all attempts to solve the hospital problem remained unsuccessful, until the abandoned wrapper of his fall and riddles arose gradually, rumors and stories about claims that they made sex their habitat for them and they are the reason that they spoil all good to run it and rehab.

The rumors were started by the source of his population in the area adjacent to the hospital, they were told about the presence of voices and noise coming from hospital lights, they added a spa and flames coming out of some windows, these people thought at first that there was no one to live inside the hospital, but when brought the company, everyone was surprised that there was nothing in the hospital. And the most unusual of all is that on some days of the holy month of Ramadan , hospitals sound fresh and raised from the mosque, but the mosque is completely closed after one access! ...

As it happens all over the world, stories of sex, ghosts and goblins are encountered by so many people, especially young men in search of adventure, who find in these kinds of stories a challenge to their courage and a means to confirm the strength and toughness of their Shechem's determination to them. In this way, the hospital was turned into a golden opportunity for exploration and adventure, as well as return visitors, secretly and openly in order to force himself to be aware of what is going on around him from rumors and rumors.

Here is an example of this story for you, dear reader.
It is said that five guys were talking on the streets of the Saudi capital of Riyadh and the king was visible to them at this time of night, said their friend who was driving the car, what do you think if we cut this file and we went to the hospital " racing, "sharing their idea with young teens, so they stopped their car in the parking lot and drove to an abandoned building looking for an entrance, and asked them to look too much, once they found the door broken, they partially walked through it, and each of them pretended to be brave.

The young people were looking for something strange, and they did not find anything on the first floor, they went up to the second floor and started looking, and someone said that I go up to the second floor and explore this floor, went up and soon after a voice of fear marched towards him on the wheel following into the room, curious where it was completely clean, smells, cleaning liquid, smells and the intensity of their attention the cup of tea was hot as molding, just then they heard the sound of feet and ran out. there was a growl behind them, but they began to disappear as they descended the stairs back to the second floor.

The grill stopped a little to catch his breath, and one of them tried to lean on the wall from the weight of fatigue, and then he was surprised to see a door behind it and an inscription on it above it (three dead), there was a window in the body with a door in it, he looked at young people through it inside and quickly screamed, his voice got scared: look !! .. They gave the beauty of the interior of the refrigerator through the window and watched how shadow people live, and they heard many voices, as if they were standing in a market or in a busy place, but they saw no one but these shadows, and then they heard a loud scream and saw three dark shadows running towards them, they fled from Harbin, but someone started screaming for help, as if someone had grabbed him and returned to the net and they grabbed his owner's legs and pulled them so hard that they saved him, and they don't know who he catches from and gets to the other side, and then they rushed to the stairs down to the first floor. where they were all running like mad along a long corridor to the door leading from the hospital, when suddenly an old woman ran out of one corridor, her features were exotic. She told them with a cry: (You woke up my animals! .. Get out) .. then on one of them and his, and ran, and my feet helped the wind.

The young people left the hospital through the broken door and they were in their steps from the weight of horror, and then they ran to the parking lot, but I met a man guarding hope in the hospital yard and shouted to them: what are you doing here this time? ...

The young man felt some consolation upon seeing the guard, and they said, "We heard there was a Goblin, so we wanted to make sure .. Wei didn't ..
Tell the guard that you must leave and never come back here. And the strangest thing that young people say is that they tried to raise the guy's mood from a transparent to a greater attitude towards

him, but he did not laugh, but smiled and changed the expression of his eyes in relation to them !! ...

The young men headed to the parking lot, where they got into their car, and they took the accelerator into a public street adjacent to the hospital, only to be face to face with the police patrol. The patrol officer stopped the young people, asked their identity, and then asked them about the reason for their presence in this place at that hour, said that they came to the hospital to verify the story that revolves around him, and apologized because they did not knew they were not allowed to enter the hospital until they were told that there was a guard in charge of hospital security whom I had met in the past.

The officer hates his dogs the most and tells them that there is no guard in the hospital and that it is completely deserted and there is no one at all.
When the guys heard the officer's words, they almost fainted from fear and swore that they saw the guard in the hospital yard, the officer went with them to verify their words, but they did not find anyone and the place was completely empty.

This is actually a famous story in the SAR community from the hospital, where it sparked a heated debate, prompting dozens of young people to enter into an agreement through social media sites to infiltrate the hospital.

And it really happened and I got dozens of young people to raid the hospital and ignite fireworks, causing damage that is actually close to an abandoned hospital in the sense of the word and the essence of the people around him, he said that some are enlarging the glass windows and modern technology in the Saudi authorities to close it completely on all sides.

Are there really ghosts in the hospital?

It seems that the answer to this question is very difficult, like all the questions that arise about places with ghosts and ghosts, simply because these things cannot be confirmed or disproved since we talk about occult and ethereal objects hidden from the eyes. But as they say, there is no smoke, there is fire, and I think that all the stories that revolve around the building, its source is the population adjacent to the hospital, these inevitably they saw the lights and heard the voices coming from inside the hospital, but not necessarily those lights and sounds emanating from sex, Don't forget that great and abandoned and places like this do not execute human volunteers for various reasons, love to explore .. stealing .. Magna's nightlife .. Drug use ... that's all there is in them. Although I am probably the first scenario, Love of exploration and adventure, the vision of this majestic building and the pumping inevitably sparks curiosity about why it remains empty for years and many people try to sneak inside to investigate its secrets and be convinced of its veracity the story that revolves around him, and these explorers come, of course, under cover of darkness to find their way inside the hospital, they have to use scout ships, lamps or mobile phones, or even hospital lamps if there is indeed electricity inside the building. This is, in my opinion, the most likely explanation for the lights seen by the population adjacent to the hospital and the sounds caused inevitably by some of those researchers of the hospital's furniture and targets, or they echo doors and glass.

Does this mean Gene was not at the hospital? ..

No, we did not say that God I know, the conditions in which ethereal organisms tend to travel to abandoned places and, for the record, the history of hospitals and inhabited products around the world, especially in the United States and England.

The amount will be pursued by the really hungry .. who knows? ...

Enter the hospital at night .. clip allegedly having a voice, garden with sex ..

The genie hangs from the ceiling of the room!

Al Cooper moved to a new home, in fact, the home was not literally new, he was almost fifty years old, but was well restored, perhaps to hide some details and things that he did not want the seller to know with his new buyers about the Black history of the product, in particular about those terrible crimes that have taken place inside it for decades, more recently about the murder of the previous owner under mysterious circumstances.

Either way, Al Cooper has moved into a new home, they are happy to record and document this happy event, pick up a souvenir photo for Cooper's sister and her husband, they are sitting in the living room with their children.

A few days later I receive the developer of the photo studio al-Cooper ...

How great was their amazement ... no matter how severe their horror was, when they first looked at the picture, this is the ceiling of the living room, where in the picture there was a foreign body of an unknown man hanging upside down and his face was not clear.

Al Cooper, they look at this creepy photo on a neighbor's old man, ask him about the history of the house, admit to the peasant that there are ghosts in the house and have seen the occurrence of many mysterious and tragic incidents.

Al Cooper left the area on a wheel the next day and the house remained abandoned for years until it was destroyed by fire and its effects completely narrowed down, everything else and the scary story is what the picture is puzzling about.

Acquisition fact

I will talk about the topic of frequency several times earlier, writing about the fact that by writing about something that is not very much, especially if we suffer, coupled with dramatically through faith in it ...

I will talk about acquisition, about the fact that the phenomenon of the spiritual that you get when you absorb an etheric person and his world by an entity other than a person and his world will keep harmless and compensate for the stages of serious physical and mental illnesses to which you most often access.

Does this acquisition really exist? .. And what is it? .. And not the types? .. And does it come from other worlds or from our souls? What is the purpose of these objects from acquiring it? ...

What is an acquisition?
Feather tips for real purchases
Faith with the acquisition of a wave once upon a time ..

I have always described an acquisition that control over the essence of a non-human person speaks of his actions and makes him see eerie visions and other natural and realistic ones to scare him away. We found that he exists in most civilizations as an idea, and all religions are grouped he exists much to the point of having a special ritual in every religion to almost ask the controlling subject ... many fossils, emoji drawings have been found to reflect this idea. Even before the emergence of monotheistic religions such as Christianity and Islam, implications of this concept existed for a long time in many civilizations of Calvin, the civilization of the Incas, the Pharaohs, and even the ancient Tibetan.

What is the quality of the objects that a person takes upon himself?
Feather tips for real purchases
There is an aura that surrounds every person, maybe objects are dimensional, others know if we were scared, worried or strong in spirit ..

I agree with the name of an object acquired on a person in this name and .. "sex" .. "evil spirit" .. "shack" to .. "gray reptiles" ... which all objects live in dimensions when they are turned off as semi-physical or virtual, they were originally raised, but despite this, their intensity ... And they are easier than they can access our world, and some of them material generally live in another dimension, as is the case with (gray, reptilian), who claim that some parasitological scientists live in the earth, and the feeling of high mental power can strongly affect the mind and aura of a person or a car, therefore forcing you to see what they want and think as they think , begin visions of whining and lack of hope for life and therefore physical and mental illness.

Okay, let's now talk about developing a spiritual cause apart from science and facts ...

I wonder at first why the acquisition is there? ... Why did God allow this? ... Why should a company be so strong? .. And why did these "if found" items turn out to be strong this time! What is his interest? ...

Feather tips for real purchases
Acquisition as an idea is based on the strength of our belief in its presence ..

Without understanding these questions, you will not know the answer only in the sense of the self and the Universe, this means self-knowledge and, therefore, the knowledge of God. When we understand this, we will know that God is merciful and that all fears come when they are no more. All evil beings or evil energies, separated from the essence and having their own dimensions, all this makes sense from our negative thinking, you must agree, arrogance, God is merciful than allowing this crime, but we made it the idea of our intentions, whether we knew it or did not know .. "the goodness of God and your souls." In other words, the acquisition of a palm tree is mainly based on the strength of our belief in its existence, which is why you see the countries most convinced of the existence of the acquisition (photo of the hills), where there are more cases of states, where the ratio of faith and spirituality.

But how can we justify this? ..

The answer is that when we believe in them, and often this belief stems from fear, we have created our association, spiritually we accept them and make them in this way controlled. Pulse shaken by oblique fear and doubt and other negative emotions whenever they become weaker and heavier, thus can be different and access to them, penetrate both according to the principle of the firewall of the weak in the computer, or as marked predators and prey, weak within the industry threaten them first. Conversely, whenever halos are more transparent and spiritual, through good work and self-discovery, be the two most powerful of them.

This begs the question: why do they want to control? .- Why did they want to scare us?
Feather tips for real purchases
Reptiles ... objects, conspiracy theorists say, they control the Earth, giving bodies to the world's leaders.

They simply kill proton energy on negative emotions, especially fear, so the more the victim loses consciousness whenever they receive their energy and therefore makes them see the fearful feelings emanating from their mind to be afraid, the more their energy gets.

There are important ideas that sound odd, but some of the forces associated with the pages of the ancient Masonic dossier are actually subject to control after these objects are acquired by the acquirer, and some of the great politicians like Henry the User or dictators like Hitler, you know what they acquire and are guided by these objects, let's take Hitler, for example, some sources that when he spoke it seemed like he was not an orator and often cried freely behind the scenes and anyone who does not know that Hitler was a vegetarian, an artist, what is that? why is a sensitive person like you selling millions of human beings ?!

There are also many conspiracies - they say that there are many experiences in the world, in fact, the wave behind the curtain and is completely controlled by objects of another dimension, without knowing it. For example, believers assert, together with the grays, that there are certain times and places of certain experiences in which secret activities are carried out to receive the "weather energy" by the objects of reptiles, and this is how he got on 11.11.2011 inside the Great Pyramids of Giza in agreement with one organization (secret order) in the presence of Obama personally as belonging to a fraternity.

Acquisition types:
1 - control of psychic energy

Feather tips for real purchases
In some cases, such an acquisition can be fatal.

As we have said, This type of object is dense for them, as we are, but their mental capacity will be high, thus controlling and influencing us, and that women make up the bulk of cases of acquisition. Much of what is said about the case of acquiring sex (Touch) in the Arab world is in fact of this type.

2 - control of the actual existence of the object

Which would be the object that actually exists at the time, was imported after through the ritual that we mentioned above, this type of acquisition is the most powerful of the species in terms of access to injury, sometimes leads to physical abuse by physical means of external stimulation or even to murder.

Of course, there are other types, but these two cases are the most common at 96%.

How can we protect ourselves from acquisition? ..
Feather tips for real purchases
The highest pulse is your path to spiritual meditation, prayer and
supplication ..

We can protect ourselves from them without thinking about them
for a long time, because the knowledge of the Universe and the
capabilities of a human being is an object of the Spirit of God,
unlike anything else. Falls in us, and they come from our negative
thoughts, why be afraid of them? Why did you let them hurt me,
huh? ... The highest pulse of your path to spiritual meditation or
prayer or supplication, regardless of your religion or your path ...
the goal is to raise the vibrations of the aura energy in order to be
fortified against them.

Usurped ghosts or genie lover?

Just thinking of genies and ghosts or hearing their stories worries many, let alone seeing these hidden creatures or being attacked by them, is something that inevitably causes fear and can lead to insanity or mental illness.

Of course, there are people who think, shaking their heads with regret, that such things happen only in our eastern countries, which lag behind the western world in terms of scientific and cultural development. The number of cinematic horror films about haunted houses, demonic touching rituals and exorcism, the only difference is that Westerners attribute these metaphysical matters to beings or ghosts of an evil demonic nature, which they call (Demon), and we attribute them to genies. Regardless of the name, these creatures are similar in many of their characteristics and the way they attack humans, as they are skilled hunters, tirelessly searching for frightened people, chasing false hearts to devour them, and chasing wobbly bodies to settle in them. .. She can smell fear in your breath wherever you are, and perhaps she can feel the beating of your heart now in confusion as you sit at the computer and read these frightening words ... Maybe she is now watching you ... and who knows what will happen to you tonight! ...

I'm sure you're now trying to convince yourself that this is just nonsense and that this will never happen to you, which is exactly what 48-year-old Debra Rawson told herself when mysterious events began to surface. in her head without representation at her home located in the English city of Hull. Once Debra was sitting in the kitchen, exhausted from hard homework, when she was suddenly attacked for no apparent reason, she felt that the air became heavy, and then felt a slight tremor in the legs of the chair on which you are sitting, and conveyed this vibration to turn towards the table next to it from the mattress and dishwasher.

What happened was puzzling and confusing ... is what you see is an earthquake? ... Debra was surprised with herself and she tried to collect her worried thoughts, but the events of the alien did not give her the opportunity to catch her breath, but meanwhile, this event is incredible, and let's use Debra, she describes it to us, saying: "a foggy cloud appeared, and I walked away back in front of the kitchen window, and slowly took this cloud, which took the form of three strange creatures, the first figure was a handsome man of about thirty in black trousers, a white shirt, and on the side of him appeared a woman, also about thirty, dressed in a pink long dress. the body shape of a child, about five years old, and has brown hair, and wears red socks, and her features looked so innocent. "

Look at these strangers who came out of nowhere to make Debra jump out of her chair and run out into the street and she screamed and screamed in the intensity of horror and then gave her husband Kevin back his job after he found out she was dressed, he asked her what about it? ... So I told him what had happened, but my wife did not believe it, thinking that they could imagine it, and asked to see her to the doctor.

By nature, a person tries to calm the splendor, convincing himself of various interpretations, when he is subjected to an ambiguous thinking in relation to the other side, even if it seems to him stupid and unrealistic, he sees how he says to himself: "let you shit .. these things do not exist only in my mind ... maybe it's just a breath of air ... or maybe it seemed to me .. I think I'm tired as a result of work. " If you venture to visit your doctor, he will finish with a couple of antidepressant pills and advice on routinely relaxing and getting away from stress and anxiety.

This is exactly what happened to Debra, she left the doctor's office and was completely convinced that what she saw in the kitchen was nothing more than a hallucination, and the result of excessive stress ... but this bomb will not last long ...

Strange things began to happen, voices and whispers of an unknown person were heard throughout the house, balls of light flew in the kitchen air. all this and the poor thing is trying to convince herself that all this is just a fantasy, but the events developed dramatically seriously, say, Debra will describe what happened.

The ghosts of a rapist or a gin lover?
Debra and her husband Kevin.

You: I was standing in the kitchen preparing food when I was suddenly hit. that sad feeling again, this time she had a strong feeling that someone was standing next to me, and soon I felt his heavy breathing on my face, so exhausted in the place of the weight of horror and screamed in a painfully trembling voice: "Who is there? And naturally, my surprised answer came to me quickly, I heard a voice from an invisible greeting: "Claire! And, after a moment's silence, the voice shouted again: "Mark here that he is watching you."

I felt like my heart would stop from the weight of horror, this time it was real, I didn't imagine, I told myself that Claire is definitely a woman in a pink dress, Mark is a guy in a white shirt, but what do they want from me , do you understand? ... And why is Mark watching me? ..

He did not ask the time, so I knew that Debra, in response to her question, a few days later, during her work in the kitchen, she felt that there is a hidden hand in the cross dress. And when she was lying on the couch in the living room, I felt something heavy in her body, as if someone was often stretched over her, and the third time she was sleeping on her bed in the bedroom, when I felt Wade envelop the subtle notes of her hips.

Debra thought that Mark was trying to rape her, she told her husband about this, but as usual she did not believe her, the pressure and discomfort must be understandable, you have to repeat the same story of obsessions on the part of the wife, relations between the spouses worsened for a while , Kevin became hot-tempered and loses his temper at the slightest pretext, and no longer sleeps with Debra in the same compartment, but began to overshadow his actions with something strange and mysterious.

The ghosts of a rapist or a gin lover?
A strange aura appears in the image of a hand-picked kitchen, Debra ..

During this period, I began to hear Debra hearing the sounds that they both come from the bathroom. One night walking by the bathroom door, I heard her husband turn his cell phone with someone else, his voice was weak, and I heard him talking about uncertain things, and I felt angry, she thought, that he is hiding something, perhaps a relationship with another woman, otherwise why is he talking on his cell phone from the bathroom in a low voice, so I decided to record his conversation on my cell phone. And the next day I appeared before him and asked for clarification about his mysterious actions recently, but he denied that he had talked to one of the toilets, and his testimony, turning to him by the receptionist on the phone, did not lag behind this sound, and soon they both sensed the terror of the tyrant, it was certainly not Kevin's voice, it was another man's voice, full of anger. and. This was the first time Kevin claims his wife is about ghosts.

Debra sign movements. increased in the following days to the point that the couple decided to leave number two and the lower staircase, but even there I did not get Debra out of the hands of Mark the frivolous. In the end, Kevin decided to enlist the help of one of the clerics to perform a ritual to exorcise evil spirits. Indeed, the priest performed the necessary rituals, and at first glance it seemed that he had managed to restore calm and serenity in the house. But, unfortunately, this did not last long, a few days after her return, strange things appeared in the house, and she again felt Debra, Mark's warm breath, and she left on her neck.

The couple decided this time to use the psychic's expertise, the bug revealed to them the secret of the ambiguity of their house, and they came to the man, and he brought his cameras, photosensitive and measuring temperature, health and politics, electromagnetic oscillations, and did not call in time until he met these devices , spotted a cool mysterious spot floating in the house, in addition to photographs of strange lights in the kitchen, and an expert witness saw with his own eyes a company pin floating in the air of the bedroom.

After that, make sure that the expert of this haunted house turned his attention to the combat history of the region, it was Debra and her husband who bought the house twenty years ago, but they never knew anything about its history, after research and discovered that the house was built in 1922 year above the land that was planted in the former, but the records do not indicate the occurrence of any crime or accident, painful and cruel through the history of the region, which is almost a century, so the shadow of the mystery of the appearance of these objects is hidden unresolved.

The expert promised to conduct a couple more investigations to solve the problem, but they were like Rush Kellner's cells, so get out of the house and Agrite each other.

Ghost sex is fun!
The ghosts of a rapist or a gin lover?
Natasha Plastic Says Ghost Sex Is Fun!

On the contrary, Debra Rosen, who escaped from her home due to the movements of ghosts, the representative of the Ukrainian uprising Natasha Plastic, says that she finds unspeakable pleasure in sex with ghosts, or any creatures of the other world, as one of the British television stations said.

Natasha says that her first non-ghost sexual experience, which happened while she was alone in her room, she described it as follows:

"I was lying on the bed in my room when I had a feeling that something had entered the room, but I could not see anything. Then I felt like someone touched my hand and pushed me subtly, although against my will and I can feel the weight of the body of lightness being determined over me. "

"I don't see anyone in the room next to me, but I can feel something pushing and hitting me, the force underneath me, pushing the stripes in different directions across my body."

Natasha added excitedly: "I liked it."

Allegedly, the ghost left Natasha for her after he took the fly away from them, but she did not leave forever, after about a month Returning to the ball again. And despite the fact that Natasha is married, but she says that the sex that she tried with a ghost is not similar in splendor to anything else that I have experienced in her life.

Natasha talked about her experience of working in one health America, said: "It was fun ... since childhood, I always wanted to know if there are other things in this world, you always ask questions, and I think it made me kind of the soothing presence of additional things that we cannot perceive with the naked eye.
" According to Natasha, her then experience of sex with a ghost gave her: "a feeling of comfort, support and answering questions about the existence of other things there."

The ghosts of a rapist or a gin lover?
Keisha, ghost sex, scared me ... open up! ...

Of course, not all of those who heard this interesting and exciting story believed her, many said that Natasha is looking for lights, an expert researcher of spiritual Alexandra Holzer says that people who have tried sex with beings from another world do not feel "warmth" , as Natasha claimed, but they get a funny experience, but on the contrary, the places where ghosts enter become cold and gloomy. "

Natasha is not only celebrities who have claimed her connection with a ghost, but on Kishi's American priest, others have also claimed that she had sex with a ghost, she said that she lived for some time in an old house and felt the presence of a mysterious energy there. that energy, or rather a metaphysically mysterious thing, was signed occasionally from her sleep during the night and soon began to take the form of a spiritually dark and greedy body.

"It scared me, but that was the funniest part of it all ..." says the quiche.

According to Keisha, her song "Supernatural" is spinning on this interface.

Of course, there are other celebrities and other stories about sex with ghost objects and specials, but that's all we expect from our all-encompassing "sex world" that we hope to finish as soon as possible.

Details of the other world

I've always had ghost-related themes that strike terror in souls and chill. As for me, my curiosity prompts me to ask more about the world and about the population (sex and evil spirits, as some call it).

Sex ... this world then ... is the world a filled space on OUR PLANET ??? .. And if so, does it have any relation to us as human beings ??? ..

I have a lot of questions in my head and I would like to reveal some of the blockages for this world. The things confirmed in the book and that the creations of God were mentioned in the Quran with the words: (come, say, turn back, he heard a group of sex). And his peace and blessings be upon him: "do not listen to shit and no bones, he has increased cousins. Sex."

Now, let's continue with some details on what the hidden world is.

What are these places where there is sex? ..
Details about another world
They live in cracks and terrier caves, in the ground.
They live sex in all parts of the earth, in caves and holes and cracks in the earth, and most of them live in vast deserts, and not in the colonies of many, and some of them live in the seas and oceans, some of them live in our homes and allow us to practice sex completely, or dwell in toilets and bathrooms (name of God) understanding demons who must beware of them.

Who are the elf kings? ...
Details about another world
Have local kings ..
Returning to one of the foreign sources, I began to offer answers to my questions a lot, and read the names of the kings of sex and I do not hide from you, I felt that the exploitation read my no, and from these names:

1 - Amon: This name may be known to some of you, it increased its name with the Egyptian god Amun, and recognizes that this file gives you knowledge of the past and future in order to offer your services to the boss, as well as in your alliance with the devil.

2 - add: he is called the destroyer, and is mentioned in the book of St. John in the name of the king of the locust, and is one of the

most ferocious demons, he is also the Supreme Commander of the previous layer of demons.

3 - ipala: this is an assistant, but it is not mentioned in only a very few books in ancient Greek.

4 - areas: the use of this name in amulets of ancient magic is also found in the name engraved on a stone during the time of Greece, and it was the pharaohs who considered him as God and a demon in one essence, and appears in amulets in the form of a wild head or a lion and a human body.

5 - Beginning: whether the king Vagin is very famous, very worried, and back to the amulets in a naked man, and not to the wings of a dragon, and is called Astarte, who received the name of the Assyrians.

6 - Lilith: And I think this is known to some of you, but under different names known in Arab countries, of which (either the burned ones or the boys) is the fairy known for dropping babies and preventing pregnancy and killing children under six and she saw our Lord Solomon on the carpet and she dropped babies and killed children, and it was said in legends that three angels and they (Sino, case, Emmanuel) brought her from their cave in Red sea, and they made her swear that she saw their names, would leave the children alone, and that is why in some cultures even to this day some mothers draw a magic circle around the child's bed and write the names of three angels and the name (Adam and Eve) and words (except for Lilith).

What are Jin's qualities? ..
Details of the other world
This is not right for all the ugly and creepy ones ..
The misconception contained in most people that they are all ugly and with thick hair, which does not correspond to the truth, the

understanding of types, including very ugly ones, and it is accepted from them that there is another type, you may not believe me if I I will tell you that they are at a high degree of beauty, human beings are white and their eyes are wide and round and their hair is long, silky.

In terms of strength, there are two tribes that fear death more than the other two (jinn and elves), in contrast to the earthly vulnerable species.

The size of the genie up to a building consisting of five floors does not mean that the sprite is weak, but whether a demon of gnomes can defeat a giant of giants, there are also types of strong ones, like those that the Egyptian pharaohs did, harnessing him to guard them, they are species deadly, and there are types that do not live on planet Earth, but in space and are called (blue) - this is the type of Vagin who have all the magic, they cannot resist them.

Types of sex:
Details of the other world
They come in different types ..
- Amer: and this is the type that lives in our homes and they are very calm Muslims who do not harm people only on rare occasions.

- Double: The demon churns out human beings from the moment of his birth to his last breath, and he called on the person to always do evil in order to say peace and blessing to him: (none of them have all their sex spouse, they said: And you? He said : "Me too, but God helped me, you became a Muslim without telling me about it, but okay).

- Genie: a type is characterized by both large and tall stature and has to do with business and magic.

-Sprite: the strongest sex categories and not necessarily in terms of size with its small size, but it has some very amazing features.

How to get rid of Jatom

Practical and 100% proven ways!

She is either a nightmare, or a night visitor, or screws, or a court, or a popper ... your tolerance is widespread in the East, in the Maghreb or in the West ... it is, in fact, a mysterious phenomenon that is difficult to define or interpret, whether then scientifically, psychologically or spiritually! ...

The scientific explanation of this phenomenon, called sleep paralysis, is a logical explanation and is not correctly denied at all, because this is a conclusion based on complex scientific experiments and there is practically no person on this earth who does not go through this experience over and over again. and I am among them! ... But the diagnosis of my knowledge was incomplete and neglected some of the points that I will mention later.

The psychological explanation for this phenomenon is also true, because physical and psychological insomnia is one of the causes of sleep paralysis and gets them ... but the psychological diagnosis is also incomplete and neglects some elements ...

Getting into folklore and religion is an abnormal phenomenon, especially when it comes to the work of another, and even more! This is true, but it also neglects some elements ...

I will give a simple explanation so as not to dwell on them, so I preferred not to draw conclusions in scientific or oil texts and verses of the Quran, because the purpose of our topic is to analyze this phenomenon, but to give some recommendations for prevention.

All interpretations of this phenomenon are amazing, but they are wrong about one thing! They explain two phenomena in one phenomenon, and each side, wanting to interpret it, denies the interpretation of the other side ... how is that?

How to get rid of the used and 100% tested!
They infect a person because they sleep in a certain place ...
Sleep paralysis is a phenomenon that affects a person, because sleep to a certain extent affects mainly the blood circulation in the head, so the type of anticonvulsant is the same as it happens to us when we sit in certain positions, one of the legs or flattened hands become paralyzed for a few moments, and sometimes I do not even feel its existence, and you get the same phenomenon with your head and brain! And, of course, fatigue and insomnia greatly affect the development of sleep, because a person is in a normal state, he is always looking for an ideal position for growth, without which he cannot sleep! But man is tired and being a snake. they often sleep very deeply, so that they even sleep in a standing position, which contributes to the occurrence of an anticonvulsant

phenomenon and therefore cannot deny the reliability of this word, but they say that this is caused by invisible beings, and that scientists do not understand this, because they do not believe in the party as believing parts and heritage of the people ...

But it is precisely those areas that have been neglected by doctors and psychologists that are the reason that this phenomenon occurs when a person is in physical health and good mental health and sleeps on a good mattress and in excellent health !!! Why such a phenomenon? Why did you observe the Egyptians as strangers and at the same time observe the people sleeping next to them and everything in the room was quickly in place and the only change is that which is strange? ... Why do you sometimes see strangers in the same place every time he and all the long years? Why is the person also in certain rooms or certain rooms, when you do not encounter this phenomenon in other places? .. why when you scream or call someone at the hospital near you, confirm it to you when you use where to ask why he didn't help you if you know he already heard you moan and emit strange sounds, but hey maybe just delusional ... that means you are not delusional and she hasn't slept! ... Own a large number of questions that do not find a convincing answer! ...

The difference between this phenomenon is as follows:

1 - Sleep paralysis of natural causes has no signs of blood flow in the brain and can be caused by a bad situation. in a dream, the source of nightmares is often seen, and dreams are not clear, as if you see yourself stuck in a hole or that someone or something heavy presses on your head, or an animal, or a person strangles you ... and to necessity take a few minutes and be so tired and jaded, and this, as I said, is very similar to what happens to the other's members when you choose.

How to get rid of are in use and 100% tested!

Possibility of being caused by supernatural or invisible beings ..
2- do or paralysis, which causes the unexplained and the most likely
to be due to supernatural and invisible creatures, and so it happens
the same as falling into sleep paralysis, but this time in an unusual
form, where a strong hidden cause of this paralysis by influence on
the members of an infected person, similar to what happens in the
case of future or damage, and in which pressure on certain nerves
or glasses in the human body or affect them after a severe personal
conflict or how to lose control in one of its members or with your
tongue ... your guide to the phenomenon that the plant wakes up
and speaks directly as soon as someone close to it touches it, while
if it is sleep paralysis, then the source will be needed Until a few
moments and seconds to wake up and again to speak in your own
body ... in this case, we do not have many reasons for this differing,
and there is a great argument, so he attributed this phenomenon to
a demon, and from them he forgot the magic ooze and evil eye or
envy, or mischievous pixie creatures ... etc.

It is also important now that everyone should know that this
phenomenon is just something fleeting, and its consequences are
the same as the consequences of nightmares and bad
dreams. Anyone that a plant feels fear and panic and pressure and
feels bad, but the most important thing is the impact of a physical
or physical person! The impact is physical and non-existent, which
simply does not have any effect on the body and not a single case
of actual asphyxiation or paralysis or death of a person is recorded,
because it is or sleep paralysis! No, and if you hear someone
mention the opposite, they bounce off the content! ..

Now we come to the stand and how to get rid of this strange
phenomenon:

- Experience confirms that this is not a person who is also trying to
get rid of and greatly change his body due to panic and the more
resistance to the increased effect, brings them to the point that

some people, when they wake up, feel some pain in their muscles, as if would they go in for the sport of weightlifting!.

- Try to get rid of it strongly and try to cause a kind of suffocating illusion in the plant by violent conflict because of the effort, and not because it does it.

- Paralysis of the tongue and is carried out where a person cannot exchange or even read the Quran.

- Panic and intense fear that accompanied this phenomenon until its beginning and after its end, which causes a kind of fear that makes the plant not fall asleep again due to the fear of a repetition of the phenomenon.

These are all the reasons in general, and the best way to overcome them is to follow the following advice and lack of attention to shit and going outside, for example, put a knife under the pillow or interest the company, or the grass, or the place of residence, etc.

- You do not need to remind yourself of the benefits of reading the Qur'an and adhkaar to sleep and sleep in a state of purity.

- For those who have a cool head and don't worry ... when you find yourself paralyzed, don't distract your efforts with muscles without peaks, calmly move your limbs as quietly as you move your finger, and then move for a second second, etc. ..you will find that your hand moves and often ends up with your whole body moving and then complete the process with the other hand.

Try to open your eyes during it, and if she saw a ghost or something near you, or perched on top of the attack, as soon as you let go of your hand, and it is true that your movement will be slow, but do not worry because it will speed up approaching him, which will make him run away from you and not come back !!! Because in any case, whether you are a man or a woman, you are always stronger and invisible creatures beat your fear and psychological impact only on them!

- We now come to the majority of the poor, that usually she returned from death or books do not age after their death - this is the world (: ... I don't care, because in a moment the situation will change a lot!

How to get rid of the used and 100% tested!
The main weapon of the gate is fear ..
The gate's main weapon is fear! The source to feel the quality of the strange fear of sudden panic he is not just like a drowning person who does not know the race, said that flop and scream and swallow water to drown yourself while if you stay calm, then give yourself and shut your mouth will float on the water ... and this is just a race! ..

Get influence you just like you can influence him on a TV with a remote control and make him change the channel or turn off the same, without approaching him or pushing him or hitting him! Imagine if television existed in a high place, and he refuses to answer correctly, what will happen to you ??? Just walking away and regretting your knees and leaving the room humiliated because you can't touch the TV or hit it! Hang your parents (: ... so get them for sure!.

The first thing to do is to stay calm, because in the first place you will pretend that you cannot get rid of your path and you knock ... follow the same steps I mentioned in the first method for determining sides and of course since you are afraid you should not open your eyes because it will definitely bring you a horror movie! Secondly, he does not need to scream and scream. because no one will help you and the most that can be betrayed about you, this groan-light will not arouse anyone's attention, especially if they are sleeping around you! Read in the Quran a special verse of the throne and that in order to get affect you are psychologically connected to you psychologically, there is no need to define your language in order to hear you and, of course, your language will be paralyzed, it is not that stupid! Reading the Quran in your heart has the same effect as reading it aloud, and here our friend cannot stop you because your remote mine has no soil to stop you from reading in yourself or in your heart !.

When you wake up and get rid of yourself, you will find that the feeling of dread is still there, and if I went right back to the people, it will be decided what happened again, and since you are still not used to limiting yourself to the troubles of another battle! Sit in your bed for just a few minutes and not out of the bedroom like flip mode and put your head where your feet are and read the chair verse and adhan tops in a whisper, of course maybe one of your parents allows you and improves poor, this is adhaan Fajra and says to pray and I am probably still in the middle of the night! ... With the permission of Allah, the Almighty will no longer return to you, and even if he does! ... With that, no problem at all! ..

To recognize this phenomenon, you need to trade several times until you reach a degree of improvement in yourself and eliminate fear, and there are also two options here! How will you convince yourself that this is a game and that this object wants to play if you continue to play with it and see its patience longer ... and be sure to tell it later, because it is impatient and will leave you, and it is easier and easier to find prey faster than you ... The second option is also useful and could make you out of the first category of owners of courage and composure, and is to think about yourself and say: "why me? Why did you hurt me? Why did he need me? Why have you trampled on my dignity? Why trample on honor and insult me in front of my wife, or my husband, or my sons, or my daughters, or my family? What can we say about your parents? My father is a coward, afraid of the shadow? My elder brother-coward and weakling, what is he on top ... imagine, or imagine that you are a guest, when people need you and respect you, and suddenly they hear you screaming at night, like a small child, and someone- then comes to find you, and finds your face whitened from pa nicki, and it is you who are improving your ideal position of wisdom and composure !!! Isn't that insult after insult ... Imagine a young man and a young lady if you are in college or boarding school there and talk to you about it several times and activate your colleagues in the room with news and become a laughing stock among students? Isn't that insult after insult? If you are a normal person, then you will absolutely get angry and feel that anger is causing you to face an entire army, not just the ghost of a coward who is afraid to make you subservient while you can, you will probably spank one! My dear brothers, this is what I advise you to think about this during the dying of quality, she rebelled against fear and won your dignity.

I'll buy you something for sure ... if you have that degree of self-control and your nerves won't need this advice and guidance, because then you will have at your disposal or your reaction will be much easier than all this ... And go on sleeping, and I think it's just a dream, you don't even need to wake up or do anything, because you'll continue to sleep until the morning, and in the morning I barely remember that he gave you something.

Finally, I would be happy to answer any query or question, no matter how simple it is, and I would also like to show you that I do not practice any conversion or slavery ... But I am just a normal person, as you decided to share with you her experience that I had for over twenty years, where she researched and read, went to UE and demons and listened to the stories of many who had the same experiences, and God knows I did not find an answer when someone, and I could not find a better cure for this phenomenon and reported that you mentioned you and that thanks to her I am not telling you that you are healed or released this phenomenon, which is still without explanation until the end of the day! But, fortunately, thanks to trading, this phenomenon turned out, which at that time I felt that this was my last watch, so that I would simply not pay any attention to the mischievous one for a moment, on the contrary, I feel a sense of fun and challenge and as if I were playing with a friend!.

Mysterious entities (1)

The image is too old to be taken 119 years ago by an amateur photographer (Oren Jeffries Oren Jeffries) in the fall of 1895 as he was out in the wilderness discovering how to use flashless photography on his camera.

As he sits on a rock near the crater of an abandoned cave in West Virginia, I hear screams that scare him, not feeling like he is running from the camera story behind him.

A few days later, usually in the company of three men, the source of these sounds was found and the camera was passed.

At the scene, they found nothing but a camera lying on the floor ..

After the acidification of the film, such a strange picture turned out! ..

In an interview with one of the local newspapers, Oren stated that these creatures are very similar to people and they are short, and he was lucky that he photographed them.

The picture, of course, is not spared the opinion of skeptics and non-supporters: some of them allegedly were able to see the reflection inside the cave and this theory is refuted by the absence of a flash or light in the chamber, while others see that they are a group of villagers or the owners of Bigfoot (Big Foot).

True to their health, Photos see in it a strong proof of the existence of worlds and times, people cannot feel it, no matter what they say about it, this picture-puzzle that eluded scientists to solve!

Genies at home

Do you feel the thrill and chills going through you when you hear talk about sex? ..

Do you know why this is happening with this? Let me tell you, but don't worry ..

Honestly, because they can stand next to you, next to you, transferring their breath to the etheric body, you are scared, you have goosebumps, they know that you are scared, they smell fear, and they also know that everywhere , wherever there is a conversation about them ... there will be fear, there will be prey! ..

Maybe you are feeling more fear now as you read these words, you are very curious to know more about them ...

Did you know that they have the same houses as we do ?.

And you know that they also eat, as we do ...

You, of course, will be interested .. Where are their homes? ......

They inhabit the homes of dark ... abandoned ... ones that no one has visited for at least 6 months.

Therefore, you must be careful with abandoned houses, and you must launch the Quran into a house that was abandoned a long time ago in order to live in it, they prefer to live in houses that do not read the Quran ..

And if I lived in a house, then they were in a corner, in gloomy dark corners ..

When they need food, they start climbing walls ..

The advantage of lightness is that the dish does not allow the uterus to eat it earlier.

And when you walk into your bathroom at home if I felt shivers for no reason ..

Make sure a goblin or demon exists ..

Let me warn you that the designed Mac is hot on the bathroom floor so as not to upset sex, it can hurt you at God's command because they don't offer to touch it. if not allowed.

And did you know that they sometimes photograph animals like the snake and the black dog ..

And did you know that types of people ... including fires ... including what causes problems ... including for blacks ..

Therefore, you should avoid books of black magic for spells and witchcraft .. it is fiddling with these books that could end his painful and confusing life ..

I read some time ago about a boy reading a dangerous magic book, despite the warning of his older brother, he saw the genie for a long time ... he ... he went to his bed and hid under the bed, and after a short time he wakes up and discovers himself strangled and his own.

And when in the morning his older brother said to him: "What's wrong with you? You didn't let me sleep all night, and I can hear you screaming" ..

Free your brother what happened and ask him to read Surat al-Bakara, which got the market on Monday, even get rid of this genie ..

Taught the little brother of the shield not to mess with sex again after.

There are many stories about sex ... and God, I know some of them may be real and some may not ..

But anyway ... be careful and stay away from anything that attracts them to the person ..

A journey into an unknown world

There are people who deny sex and some of them are skeptical and they persist in their existence, plural name, one pound, two objects dominate with firearms. They are capable, in a whole or a class of them, displacement in various forms will be a bat, if in their true, you see more than the original, two minds are aware of its conscious and have the ability to do hard work that delights their we-humans.

Sex objects with her powers are super enjoyable, and don't mind the fact that some objects are cute unlike other types of private sex and be capable of miraculous break-ins ..

To the world, including placing secrets to numb minds and thoughts ... The Good God made a great proposal, but some people have used the sexual state in deeds of evil and destruction, as well as sabotage and massage with black magic of ferocious evil.

And to you, dear readers, a few short stories that we have collected from the stomachs of books about those who scoffed at sex and sparked them with their world of the unknown.

Miracles of Dr. Salmon
A journey into an unknown world
Salmon .. he was a witch of spiritual strength, despotic ..

He passed through our country, a stranger shot in the same name (salmon), showed on his hands some miracles of magic, hypnosis and his spiritual transformation, and therefore carries some sports, followed by the magic of India and Tibet.

The fact is that he put into the hands of the late Saad Zaglul Pasha, who was then the Prime Minister of Egypt, Cuba, empty of aluminum, and continued to see each other until the load in Saad Pasha's hands began to carry it, and put him out of his hand.

And that he buried himself underground for six hours in the city of Alexandria in front of a meeting of doctors, and then got out of there alive, and at the same time the person dies, after a few minutes if he lost his breath in the fresh air.

The fact is that this is a bedroom, but there is no broker, they talk about a certain man who was absent for twenty years from his family, they said that he lived in the Upper Town, for sure, and he has a store there, and he married the daughter of the store owner , so he died, he began to dispose. He gave his family his number in their personal account and your connection with his parents.

Adorable face of the tribe
A journey into an unknown world
Your father worshiped this idol ..

He lived at the beginning of the century as the face of a tribal witch, and asked people to put boats in the sea, and if they did, they returned to them, and more than that, so Matthew wanted his son to practice his craft, and when his mother this asked, so he asked her why she opened (the wheel) and an idol came out of it, and she told him: your father worshiped this idol to help his demons in the wonderland show, please make sure that like Kafr is yours father.

A witch in the era of the guru
During the reign of Sultan Al-Guri, the Sorcerer's level appeared, where the hands of the accused were like those of a heretic witch, and he did voodoo with yogurt and Earth, not so contrary to the law of Islam, and sent him to the next Maliki, proving the validity of the accusation attributed to this person , and he himself was an unbeliever, and ordered to hit him on the neck, waving it around him under the office of the school gym, after which she was naked on a camel.

Magic in India and Tibet
A journey into an unknown world
Dalai Lama (XII) on his throne in Tibet .. land prices

Published the newspaper (the Mokattam) in its issue of December 21, 1933, a profile of a psychiatrist doctor (Alexander) translated from a book into print in a London psychiatric hospital, and this book (the world is not evolving).

Came to this digest the reality of two freaks (magic) and I remember in the following these:

1 - the doctor had the aforementioned acquaintance (professor), a knowledgeable Sufi, an Indian, the professor was called a visit to the doctor by the mystics of India, then the visitor discovered that he was talking a tree, a fig, saying: well done ... her, Anna had the time of your departure from this world, the world of vanity and

insignificance, do it now and never come back to life. People are fucking off, but the doctor found her dead! ..

2.the doctor's income, transferred to the (Lama) of the Tibetan, was needed by the greatest of the sages - and he found when eight people were carrying the coffin, then they also lifted the lid and saw the person mentioned by the doctor who looked like a dead man, allowing him (the lama) to scan, so that the pulse and heartbeat of his heart was felt , and he was stone cold, his eyes were the eyes of a man who had spent the whole day at his death. Attaching the mirror to her mouth and nose, and without showing a trace of implementation, that is, the words of the lama, we saw how the dead man opened his eyes and then sat in the coffin, two priests helped him to get up and walk, but the man returned to his original state through two hours . And these are just optical illusions from sex, because no one is able to revive the dead, not the same God he was to become the witch Immortal, but this black magic is called the Magic Eye, where the horse is alive for them.
Sex has symbolic meaning
A journey into an unknown world
They found the smell of oil in the tea.

In the December 1958 issue of The soul magazine, an article appeared titled (Spirits drive us out of our home), which said that the author does not believe only in materialism, but believes in something behind them, until he and his family are something happened that made him believe that the world is invisible. To summarize, on the evening of August 1958, he surprised his family by visiting oil (kerosene) and eating and drinking, and there are a lot of activities, but this phenomenon was never interrupted, and they found brewing tea in electricity in oil too.

On the day of the paper that appears above the screen, tear it off and do this: (leave the house beautiful) ..

And several times they warned about the leaves again, and finally threatened to burn down the house if they did not come out, and after a few seconds they found smoke coming out of the closed compartment, and not one, opening it, hit the fire, and they did not go out, resumed another house fire, so they went out over subversion, and after living in another house, they knew that some pride residents in their city could have the same thing happen to them as happened to them, so I meant them in the bucket on I am still a riot in their house, so they went to someone for whom fasting for seven days and the treatment of an employee has its own style, and on the seventh day they found a paper teapot with the inscription: "Go home in the morning."

And they did it and went for the riot of the product.

Photo fantasy magic and witchcraft
A journey into an unknown world
Learn to even lose sight of ..

We did not film the crusaders in Damietta during the reign of Sultan Saladin, besieged them for thirty-five days and the Wolf as inspirers, then we had to visit tea, please go to the sea, and down the field, big, Damascus, we saw many fighters and various players, and maybe someone came to whom the person of the center of the nervous system offered to show us the miracle of witchcraft, then don't do it.

Erecting a tent in the field between the hands of Sultan Salah ad-Din, and like a ball of rope, tying a thread in his hand, and then strongly sending the ball to the sky, then you know that he went up even in the wrong direction, and then he fell between the people alone from his feet, and crawled until he entered the tent, then landed with one of his hands and entered the tent, as the other did, and then the remaining limbs fell down one by one until the head fell into the tent, then through an hour a man from the tabernacle and had a full member at that time, and towards the negative and the earth between his hands, since the people were like that, he entered the tent, the second before the fire, the man, accompanied by those present, said: "Get into the tent and look there ", but they did not find anyone, then untied the tent, they advised her to get out of the guy walking on her own feet somewhere else, this is a wonder to his people.

But we will put the prince to kill the demon, and crush his neck among the people, and tell King Nasser: "this is how I do not believe to be a spy of the Crusaders," and then he wanted to kill his companion, her bored Nasser claimed that she did not know him before, and nothing improves on what he did. He told Al-Nasser: "Take this watch out of Damascus, and not what he will tell you," went out of his watch. It was stated that the son is not one in his history.

Ibn Battuta and the air engine
A journey into an unknown world
The Indian rope trick is still practiced even today, there are many interpretations, no, but it is not known exactly how the magician by .. look in the picture .. the rope hung in the air and the boy climbed, but he has a regular rope ..

The air motor is a whole series of witches witnessed by their famous traveler Ibn Battuta during his visit to India, China, who stated that he was not a party to tell them where he himself witnessed how the bewitched in amazing, mind-blowing ways use blinding. This is stated in connection with this:

"And that night, a demon appeared, who from the servants of the law said about the Prince:: Show us from miracles that he took the ball has a hole in the CEO everything, he was thrown into the air, free even missed the path, we are in the middle of days of intense heat why don't you hold the sword in your hand, but a little fun not to do it, then she went into the air to be missed; let him not answer him three times, he took the knife in his hand also and the disc to be missed too, then throwing the boy's hand on the ground, then throwing his leg, then on the other side, then with the other leg, then his body, then his head, then fell, then he protrudes and his clothes stained with blood before the ground between the prince's hands, and the Chinese, and there is a prince of something, then he took the boy's members, so that he straps some order in the leg, said Together, But of them, striking my heart with trembling, like what happened to me when the king India, when I saw it in this way, fornicates me, the medicine leaves me that I have found.

The boat was the most exquisite duty on the side, and he told me: God, that was from the ascent and descent, and a member of the cut, but this is a feeling. "
Magic Eye
A journey into an unknown world
A stranger entered the city ..

The son is not also the fact that during the reign of the king of complete Ayyubid someone drove from Morocco to Egypt, and scientists (especially customers) "magic" showed someone from the objects a grove outside the base of many fruit trees and five service drivers promise there reality with streams, and an orchard stood around it. When he saw that the guy from the items he likes is buying his Moroccan thousand dinars and his jewel and you have to go in front of the judge to get an orchard out of it and the buyer in the grove he bought, so he ended up among the sand dunes, and did not see anything from that orchard that sold it to a non-Moroccan, he asks: "Have you been here in the garden until today?" And he says, "what we heard about it." Usually they ordered it among the people, and he had a complete dossier of this Morocco, but they did not find it, but took a thousand dinars and went for it.

Said, the son of the Yemenite kings, gave them a complete file of brass candlesticks made by men from a brazier when dawn broke, and the king said to him, "Good morning, God, come out at dawn." Or, from the whistle of this meaning, it was preserved as a candlestick until the time of King an-Nasir Muhammad ibn Kalawun, and then it was lost.

We had a strong heart and stay tuned
After that I got to know these facts that we have provided, please, to be strong in your mind and your soul and your faith in God in this universe, and watch to read the facts and their equipment, such as who they read about electricity that they kill and kill, and those who read the news of earthquakes, volcanoes, lightning meet terribly as they read it and are not annoyed by the fatal lightning strike and sudden mass destruction; so keep track of what you read about sex or what you read. on the other hand, or what you hear from accidents, it can God protect humanity from evil, the laws of sex are known only to God. And they do not receive damage only very rarely, we rarely hear about their realistic accidents in a few years, while we hear from time to time about accidents, earthquakes, floods, lightning, meteorites, used electrolyte.

Just like in the evil, but Winnie Hairat days, scientists and the well-being of clients, doctors and therapists, since it was God who created every disease with a medicine This was done for both sinister relationships, and what comes from the spark of sex is the purpose of the sermon ...

30 facts you might not know about genies

I offer you over 30 information about sex and some of them about demons obtained by search engine (Google), and I would like to collect you in one ..

Before we start the feet of the devil and my God, (the name of the merciful God) ..

So, here's the information for you:

1.there is a goblin called Sex World, if you change your clothes, say that Bismillahi God does not even see the nakedness of the look of his malignancy.

2. she is a being of sex, standing right behind you, even when you sleep, and when the dream sits on top of you and tells you that what she read in itself before bed will do you good.

3-Sex about you a day if you mention the name of God.

4 - beware of planting pins and nails on puppets, Yes, dear reader, a puppet or a puppet can be pursued or possessed, the last command is an evil revenge.

5. Do you know you can want sex when you speak out loud and you hear it as an echo of your voice.

6-After the middle of the night, don't walk around your house a lot, because this time is their time.

7.Crying alone pushes your partner to hug you, which is why you sometimes feel a sudden rise in temperature.

8-You mentioned the name of God when you throw things and hot water in the bathroom and when you jump from a high place, because there might be jin sleeping wand from you.

9-If the devil does not lie next to the sleeping person on his right side, and he cannot burden in his dreams even to change his sleeping position.

They say that when you smell fire, there was no fire anymore, now I know that sex was next to you, because they were created from fire.

11. We also have peoples and tribes and their world as our states and your religions.

12 - sex cannot hurt someone, ruler of adhkaara.

13 - You may have to have sex to hurt you if you are alone in the house with sounds and movements to keep the terror in your heart.

14 - do you know what slag is, what is the unity of Allah, what is it? ... The slag male unity of Allah is female, entering the bathroom, say: "I seek refuge in you from the slag unity of Allah."

15 - this is communicated by the mind, sex is not so welcoming, for example, the sex of my adult will be his mind, like the mind of a child of 10 years old.

16 - there is no person who does not need Paradise, never, sometimes, meet a strange person, he is a person, but in fact he is a fairy.

17 - be careful when you call someone after midnight, if you don't get a response from us, it will be your sex and he wants it.

18 - If you suddenly stumble upon an animal looking for them, how do you know if the kilograms are or not? Scare him, and then

innocently look at you and make sure that kilograms of jerky are disguised in the animal's body.

19 - you are not alone priapism This place is creeping from right and left to south and north.

20 - When you hear barking near you, check to make sure there is a goblin in front of you.

May 21st is sex in your love and being close to you all day and stays with you comes to you in a dream in the form of a friend.

22-they say that spouses don't sleep, seem to be walking around the room where you sleep, and perhaps throw something on purpose to wake you up if I'm bored.

23-pressure after midnight, strongly denied by a demon named "cube", which remains with you even the cause of your crying at the same time and strength.

24-when you enter abandoned places, do not joke or laugh, because the sex life of those places that do not leave him.

25th spouse does not die. but stay on your grave until the Day of Resurrection.

26-when you hear songs, dances, sex, demons around you.

27 - you suffer from the fact that the membrane in Royer's eye interferes with the Angels and without this membrane enable a person to see everything that is hidden from us.

28. When you wake up between 2 and 3 o'clock in the morning, there is a high probability that some creature is watching you.

29-sex is everywhere not responding, if someone is reading this article with you now.

30-they next to you look at what you read about them and smile .. read it found yourself now for that and you.

Horror cocktail

one . families of fugitives:
Horror cocktail
In short, these were the families of criminals ..
Over that city is not harsh in recent years, when the impact of the first hurricane during the flight of people from the city on ships, real estate and other things towards the second for safety, the number of people they see, people with their families for the first time they (men, women, as well as children and young girls), they leave some rooms of the houses a lot, to some extent they escaped with people from the hurricane.

In particular, the number of fugitives, the eldest of whom knows that they are not people, but the city is small, and people know each other.

As soon as they left people's homes, out of nowhere, in short, the Jin families heard the news about the hurricane and gravity, the fugitives came to survive, and if they knew about sex, they did not try to tell anyone about their real or offended, guided by the principle of compassion for all, and also to prevent the spread of terror among the people.

Tell me the story that it was already with the venue, and he sees people, sees them for the first time, families of many discussed classes and the population of the city is growing

Crazy, but I had no idea he never, they weren't human.

2 pound wedding meal:
Horror cocktail
Not only the kilograms, I took the slaughter from their food ..
In the midst of a celebration of men and their art at a wedding in one of the NATO villages and some men who allow him, they saw an unidentified woman made available for cooking and processing in the middle of the valley on the ground, and I took a large bowl of slop and went out, men began to call her, and she does not want them, there are those women who go to the farmer, and not to the houses of the inhabitants of this village, it is not any of them, terrorizing these men, and they were not the only pounds that I took from them from food, so much of what was seen before and after it happened in the same place.

3.Tax disadvantages of goblin schools:
In the nineties, a theater party was held at the boys' school of the night, two or three with a play went into the darkness and moved

away for a while, and they said that it was as simple as turning off the lights, opening them and throwing stones at the page.

When I returned to one of the countries after the end of the concert, as soon as I opened it for my room, dumbfounded by what was above the fan hall, I looked at him angrily and, frightened, tried to run away, but out of the acuteness of fear I crashed into the door of the room, reassured him with his head, fainted and was taken to the hospital after waking up there, telling them the full details of what had happened.

4 - Range Rover left (Land Rover):
This is a British war industry policy, similar to those used by local African safaris, or those used by waste guards on their patrols, as used in wars in some poor countries, it consists of a cabin chair, two or three at most open drawer at the back.
Here I give you two opportunities to tell me about it, about its author:

- The first bus: someone's long-suspended Land Rover in the sand at night, and its owner was then alone, and when, while trying to get rid of it, he pressed the gasoline pedal, he felt that the car was not moving in a heavy direction, immediately looking back was a big disaster! He saw three people appear out of nowhere, and they pulled the back of the car, and quickly pressed the gas pedal, so hard that he managed to get rid of them.

- Case II: two men went to put their fishing tackle on the shore to bring barrels of fuel for their car at night, and when someone tried to get the barrel out, he felt a terrible chill that ran over him, and when he returned to the car and asked the owner for what - for some reason not to bring it, the barrel did not answer him, and during the run their car did not turn on - heavy, as if someone had caught it, part of the driver pressed the gasoline pedal hard and opened with difficulty, and when I moved, then he heard the sound of gasoline pounding hard on the glass. and they peel off the wrappers left and right, and he tells his companion that he felt the presence of sex as soon as he entered the store and eventually deprived them of them because we pissed them off so that they could barely pull out your cars and run away from them.

5 - Horror Village House:
Horror cocktail
An unknown woman was found in the courtyard of the house.
A long time ago, one of our relatives entered our village house for the night, and found an unknown woman in the yard of the house free and ran away irrevocably.

The same house, another cousin entered one night to get his clothes and flight instruments of his fleet, and during his presence the room is dark, I heard two women outside talking to each other and saying to him: Son of this ?! sneaky close to this, part of the wolf on the run, I knew this from the FBG of our village behind the house in the village, and in those people who neither live in one, and I think I will not forget soon and will not try to repeat the experience alone again.

And now the bird from my stories will attack ** don't look for it in stores !!

Hoping to get back to ** survival rope fashion.

Worshiping Both Worlds

Question: Who doesn't like this ?? We all love and cherish, whether we love him and his person of the same sex or the opposite sex, may not love him as much as we call work ... and also love people who are notorious in the art world. sports, literature, because of their actions.

But this is very strange and illogical - to be love there not between each other, but between two different worlds and not die together, there was no connection ... and by this word I mean love between a man and a demon.

I have read many stories about people (especially girls), they claim to be adored by sex and have sex, and they want to marry and bond with them, these kinds of stories inspired me and puzzled me at the same time, how can a transparent low density being rise to a more intense one? But first, let's move on to some of the things that were similar between our world of us humans and the world of sex:

1.Every member of the worlds has a family and the clan varies from one person to another.

2. Each of us has a system of government led by a person who is responsible for him, protects him and takes care of him.

3. all worlds have their own rules and special rules and strict control over their world.

4 Each of the worlds created the slaves of Allah.

What differs across the worlds is:

1.Every member of the world of sex must be stronger than the strongest person in the world because of the energy that he owns.

2. people are much smarter than sex.

3. they all live in a world facing the world, and one can go to another world only with the help of charlatans and / or some spells.

Despite the fact that all these things are like-minded and diverse, in fact there is love between the worlds, most of the time there is this love of one side, either side for sex, and it is for the lover of sex.

I think we all know who the sexual world is, this is the kind of sex that loves to build welcoming veils with its beauty and its bodies and haunt them, often speaks to them and sets them free for their own interest, and that the ends of the ransom are looking for another sacrifice to do to her what her predecessors did.

Let's admit Some of the things that sex does with a girl who is obsessed ....

Loves sex my Medial or love Fairy Medial as it happens between the sons of Adam adoration and admiration, it is clear that the one who loves in the world that people face Hassan thin skin white skin, it was said: "the white half of Hassan, but this gold is not finds in the world of sex, even if all this is the end, when sex has not remained dry in the body of the possessed after that he is older and feels his head and his face and dripping teeth, and adoration is actually one of the most difficult cases of a proposal, a very insoluble case difficult to find". persuade from the outside and factories, thanks to the saturation of the sexual body with love for humanity, especially if the source in fasting is from the remembrance of God.Many demons do not like possessed people, but their love for the flesh, they eat and drink and enjoy, and they do not care about people, be it happy or sad, it may hurt you, and serve a magical eye, or it simply violates the personality of the university fighter. These are symptoms of what is often with the adored holiday in the vigilance day and night, and can feel adored, who follows him and hugs him without being noticed, and can deliver will, cannot in war or conflict include those who oppose his "murder" is awake, not asleep, as in an episode involving a modern full "gets penetrated", if he completed his sleep and woke up, he found himself tired, as is the fact that the patient is sleepy at any time at work or at school and studying , the devil flows in the method of moving at the beginning of it in the house, Sometimes a displacement in the image of a man or woman who knows her medial and sprinkles in your house at best a picture of approaching, are absorbed by the floor, and some people enjoy the fact that the foreplay is intended for to make horses and their release work and sleep quickly, maybe they see that spectrum of beauty.

From the point of view of many, that is, his love for sex, you must help him quickly and bring about a catastrophe that will come to you, even if the Medial does not want it, the feta advanced to the person reading the Koran, to you and to the house, and poured water on him source and other things.

Man and genie .. When man turns into prey

Is man an easy prey for the creatures of the other world?

What does the genie want from a person and why does he always seek to dress him and harm him, why do genies hate people and what is the reason for this hatred and hatred, and is a person an easy prey for the creatures of the other world or can he resist? ... Why is a person afraid of genies? ..

Perhaps the answer to these questions lies in the nature of the jinn, for it is possible to resist the object that you see and see, but to resist a mysterious and invisible creature is very difficult and creates terror in the soul.

Why can genies take revenge on people?
The genie is associated with a person in the belief that a person intentionally harms him, and a person can harm these creatures without knowing about it, and harm to a person looks like this:

1 - Screaming, crying and singing in the bathroom, because the bathroom is a favorite place for genies.

2 - Harmful to cats, dogs, crows and some animals that may already be a genie shaped like an animal.

3 - Reading magic books and trying to summon souls like Ouija and other things.

4 - Jumps from a height without calling on Allah, so he falls on a sleeping or lost genie.

5 - There is a genie of evil origin who, unnecessarily and without justification, causes harm to a person.

6 - Accidental killing of the descendants of one of the jinn leaders, such as his children and sons.

For information, the genie sometimes tries to rape a person and it works very well, and some genies adore human girls and harass them while they sleep. The genie can also kill a person if he wants to, but he cannot harm someone with a strong will and faith, and he often looks for weak prey and prey psychologically and spiritually.
Goblin mirrors
Often Rose reflects a story of sex, especially a sex lover, but what is that story? ... Don't you have any signs of sex? .- And we really see everything as we think? ..

Someone might say that mirrors not only show us the reflection of our images, this is true, but not our vision for something other than the reflection of our paintings does not mean the absence of something else, some of them said that mirrors - it is the gateway to the worlds that throw us things that we do not enjoy the feelings of the small and are aware, we cannot see everything, why do we not see behind the walls? ... And we can see some colors or radiation, because they really are the same red and ultraviolet ..

The palaces of senses and limited understanding explains why we cannot see another world, and why we cannot see ourselves in the mirror, while other mirrors in our house may be ghosts in the part where we do not know.

Due to the adhesion of mirrors, the other world has increased since the leg to foot in folklore, where there is a fairy-static in the mirror tells them about things invisible.

Sex lover what does he want?
Can you break us for this love? I'm generally friendly about sex, but these terms are mentioned in religious books and heritage. And male sex in the following form:

1.Enjoy While Asleep: Where To Enjoy Sex In Human Beings Without Feeling Like While Asleep.

2 - Cal Gas Visible: Feel the person who is suffering without being able to stop him.

3 - saturation in the form of a man: believe it or not, it has the form of sex in public places or groping a man, likes to meet a man, see his wife and vice versa.

The sexiest world to be a kind of sex pilot is too much bitchiness and messing around with people because Amer pounds any habitable house. As a result of everything we said earlier, we can:

1 - Sex can calibrate women.

2 - women can enjoy sex, but they feel and see.

3 - If you shape sex in the shape of a human being, then it can deprive a virgin girl, this rarely happens.

4 - sex without form can calibrate a woman, but without the space of her virginity.

Types of sex are different their recipes

Sex Scan: This type only registers Muslims and they are children and grandchildren of sex and they talk about types of sex in general, including princes and kings, and there are very few of them.

Lunar Sex: This type is 80 percent Muslim and 20 percent demons and is capable of optical gambling mating between them and their ferocious fighters.

Sex firearms: the main types and they have sex there, it was not any kind that existed since the creation of the sex and belongs to them, the devil damn it, there is a cut of them called devils, and people and tribes of the sex are blue and red and green and that the tribes dominate children of the devil. This type represents more than half of the sex in the world, Kfar is more of a Muslim, this type is characterized by many and they look very scary. this guy used the motorcycle fanning style if he wanted to catch a human body, and that's their favorite patient Fischer's way of getting warm where Genie is.

Sex water: they went to live in the sea and bodies of water of this kind by groping a person during the race and a lot of this kind of sex doctors.

TRAPPIST Jinn Earth: The Living Earth and can this kind of development in the ground so fast, and they are of the shorter kinds of sex in terms of height where they look like dwarves and possess The humans a lot and sometimes staying home and waiting for them.

Sex aerobic sex is good: types of sex rarely affect a person, and if the Messiah is partial, then this is not a risk, which we called good, because it is less types of sex Download, it does not move like the rest of sex, and the risk is in the fight kinds of ideal sexual water, because it is weak in the ability to limit it in the sky.

Man is not easy prey.
A person considers himself to be an easy prey, but you must not forget that these are even more objects that we identified with God and the person had a strong faith, it is difficult to have sex in anything, and I hesitated to see him or meet him, he will be very weak and nothing can do with a person a strong faith in God is the one who created the genie and created the reason for everything, that being with us is such an object.

Why are you afraid of the wolf?
We have often heard and know that sex is afraid of animals like the wolf. The question is, why be afraid of such a powerful creature as the sex of a wolf? ..

The reason is that the wolf, when he sees the floor, does not distract him for a second, does not take his eyes off the floor, and the secret for this is that the measuring system, if you look closely at the fairy, he cannot leave the office. because looking at them, they live, and FYI, the Wolf is the only animal that can prey on sex if it is formed on the body of the animal. Some scientists argue that the wolf can kill sex because of the ability of the wolf Haka to conquer the floor, and this ability manifests itself in his eyes, which do not lose their luster even after his death. But there is no evidence that the wolf can feed on sex for the whole truth, but they claim that it can feed on it if mixed in the body of an animal or human.

Sex and saturation
Sex likes too much risk for a person to lose is formed on the body of cats, dogs, snakes, and the most famous animal has from the body exactly a sector, and the other, which shows the shape of a black

cat, but does not, for example, the female sex in saturation in the body of Gatos bright colors .

How do we know if a cat or animal is skeptical:

1 - Find an animal that is opposite to its nature, for example, some cats are shy, but gender makes them not attack people.

2. Look at yourself for a long time and, oddly enough, you will find that the animal looks at you strangely, like a person, just like you.

3. Change its qualities and color, for example, if a black cat is embarrassed, become a blacker cat.

Marriage sex
The life of sex is close to our life as human beings, so they have their own love and feelings, hate, and they have a ceremony, a ritual, especially in their marriage, their marriage age is somewhere between 200 years, since it owns pound of feminine hymen as a human woman and a guide in her honor. Give birth as
a fully human woman and can take a number of dates and sex for more than one party and leave them and take care of them can bring up the age of a fully human.

Man

Al-Zohari:

The human key to treasures hidden underground

Nadia was a six-year-old son with her brother on her way to a school about 2 miles away from their home. At the same time, a black color with a bottle of smoke stopped next to them, which darkens vision. Disarming a stern-tanned man in Sofia's clothes was like wearing Moroccan clothes usually on cold winter days.

Kill the man from the club a little, and then take out of my pocket 50 dirhams coins to quickly put them in his hand, and he checked his palm well, and then looked into the eyes of my club, as if he was looking for something that I I do not know ... he said, saying: You, my Child, buy them sweets, and do not forget to give them to your brother.

She just stood still and did not say a word, and then put her hand in her brother's hand, and the two of them ran away, because their mother always warned them not to trust strangers, not to walk with them and not accept anything from them, but the man was quicker from the two of them.

Man Sees: The Key to Human Treasures Hidden Underground
The man put his hand on the girl's mouth and kidnapped her.
As soon as a man put his hand on the mouth of the club, and vigorously, every now and then he threw it into the hollow of his black one. The car moved off at a breakneck speed, leaving behind him a little brother shouting with all his might: "Nadia was kidnapped by a man in a white coat."

Signed news about the people of the club and the Thunderous value of the parent company and the moves begun to catch the kidnappers and find the missing girl, the first hypothesis developed by the family for the disappearance of the child who is the club "above" may be behind the disappearance of the treasure hunt groups that await at every delay region.

Confirmed the family's doubts after revealing that there is a headless child's dead body lying at the edge of a nearby forest.

The mother escorted the police to the place where the head of her daughter Nadya, who had returned to her, was found, despite the terrible scalp skin and a broken one of her pupils, which was next to the body of her clothes, which were seen last time.

The history of the club is not the only story that happened to children who carry the qualities of the zone, the relevant data is replete with similar stories about people who saw how they had one of their organs amputated or carried out a massacre at the hands of people blinded by greed and the desire to access wealth easily said that they drive them crazy, kidnap innocent children and subject them to various types of torture, and not for the sin they have committed, only they carry the qualities of the zone, which are jugglers and charlatans in their blood, to sex that is guarded treasures and cabinets.

You may be wondering, Dear reader, what is the meaning of this word? What tends to see from other normal people?

Man Sees: The Key to Human Treasures Hidden Underground
The adorable need for a kid's area to get to the treasure
The word she in Moroccan comes from the word "throw" flowers, which in Arabic means "luck".

Perhaps the word Mark wrote "Zuko", which is one of the most important books, Israelite and Jewish, which dealt with the philosophy of the "Kabbalah", is one of the most dangerous magic books of the Hebrew and the book of the development of writing Zuko. Whatever the value in the folk culture of Morocco, this is a person who will be lucky to the maximum, because all the things of this world will be soft and open in front of him, the chosen God from among thousands of people to ignite good luck on the paths of life http .. But the grace of good luck , these often turn into a curse on their owner, because people see death often marked by their ghost in every place will be a shock for the powerful family when you find that God the living child holds the sign or signs of the "kind", because he sings about his happiness and live, he doubles his responsibilities significantly in control and all the crocodiles that lie in anticipation of their child and threaten his life.

Signs of the human zone
The human look is a person, when, according to your ability, you can make it a link between the world of sex and the world of humanity and its relationships ..

- Be adorable with any kind of straight blowjob to cut your tongue all the way down.

- Palm of the right hand or the left or those with which there is a straight line and cut it randomly (like in the picture).

- His eyes were with them near the light so that the right eye falls slightly into the left eye.

- Blood color is light for coloring common knowledge.

- There is a special glamor in his eyes and everyone sees how they are noticed.

- The status of your company 'palms' in the Moroccan dialect is such that they are V-shaped in front, either of the houses of the people of the first front above the eyes, or not two people at the top of the head, as in the picture.

Rarely are the other signs involved in jurisdiction magic, and they come tangentially associated with the comfort or belly of the leg.

Man Sees: The Key to Human Treasures Hidden Underground
There are physical signs especially in the children's area
The color can only be seen in his eyes, or in his hands, or in his head, and I was in several relationships, that means he is confident in first class and this is a kind of request for sex, demons and if the treasure was huge and old too.

A person sees where the blood goes, I do not drool the researchers behind the treasures hidden underground in front of its floor who they are, how there are charlatans and charlatans in fashion who believe in the abilities of this child, who is not chosen into the dirt by people, so that the offspring of the sex simply was replaced when his boy is born from a man's son ??? !!! To do this, you need to have this special closeness to sex and not be afraid of them, as well as to intuitively see things highly that you do not realize as your normal person, he does not have the opportunity to explore the location of the treasures buried in the bowels of the earth, to understand the end of extraordinary people, they sometimes see things that are not visible to a normal person, since this does not affect where the magical world is and take them by eye.

And always in popular culture, a person will see who can kill from the treasures of the sex they have appropriated and loves it in his hand without any harm, even a lovely boarding house, or any person for this will be severely punished, can cost him less life than oil in the distant place (according to their beliefs).

The cobweb needs flowers most of all exactly where the zone should pass over the place of the treasure in order to calm the army guarding the treasure.

This category of children is hunted by witch doctors to grant treasure protection permission to inventors of, after all, various varieties of treasure and jewelry. The deal, which the council sought through the cooperation of the fathers of the children's families, was aimed at fear, torture and murder.

It was known to Morocco many cases of disappearance of a large number of children, see rape, abductions occurred in some cities rich in the treasures of Kemer Marrakech war and tick.

The TV program knows about the tragedy of some families in which her children were kidnapped.

Consort the hidden enemy of man

Every person has a village that sends their devil when you go abroad into the world of your mother's womb.

He said (I was in disregard of this Revealed to us about your cover for a lot ... their spouse said, that's all for Atida were thrown into hell every Kfar stubborn areas for supported suspicious you do with God another God paid in torment extreme said the consort, who is the lord of aging, but he was far from misleading he said that we were not presented to you and what seems to say I am and I am far beyond that.)

These verses tell us about the spouse and his promised man in the world, Muhammad, and that humanity will be possessed — one torment.

This is someone hanging on every human being a Muslim and a liar he is a boxer a person who followed me everywhere was wasted on a person accompanied either in a dream or at work or in prayer and not obscenity can cause a person's anxiety and fear and anxiety, a man is not a village woman, not your partner.

Consort is man's hidden enemy
This is a creature of the upper layers of the sex, which is tenacious and strong.
Who is Karin?
This creature from the thinnest layer of sex powerfully used both its service qualities and anger.

The spouse does not burn or die because he is connected to the
foundation in this world, and God creates to complete
the comparison and equation between the next person or lie.

Consort Foxy and cunning, he looks like a man in his actions and his
voice and intonation and has a great influence on human dreams
and this makes a person remember milk or forget it

The consort basic function:

Test the servant of God whether it's true in obedience to God or
not.

Smart Consort:

If you control his brain hidden on the human mind, not familiar
with big changes, and his cells become a human block of the month
and plunge into it voluntarily.

Consort is to say when you hypnotize a person magnetically, who
plunges into the depths of any human being in front of you and you
to God, or feel your own relief or disgust when betel nut is with
your ex.

See consort:

Can you see how your partner easily walks up to the mirror and
looks at images that are similar to you, but upside down, this is
your double, similar to you in profiles and photos, but this is from
the world of sex.

Be careful when lengthening your gaze in the mirror because it
hurts your spouse, thereby hurting the person.

Consort is man's hidden enemy
Women also have their gender peers
Spouse Information:

1-cry alone pays the spouse, then this is what causes the height of your body heat when you cry.

2 - the consort is awake, but walking around the room you sleep in has to sign something when you get up, so if you're bored.

3 - the consort never cries in his life and kills at the death of his master.

4 - If you got into a big fight, and this person fell ill with one who fell shortly after, then it may be because of a partner who went to take revenge on you.

5. A whistling sound in your ear means your partner is trying to speak to you.

Check with your spouse if this is possible?

As much as possible when you are sitting alone and talking to him. ideas can change who answered this yoga

Where does a spouse go after a person's death?

The function of a spouse is obsessive, and the temptation and death of the human task is fulfilled, the spouses go where God wants them.

After all, you should know, dear readers, that you cannot be your partner, your friend. he is a demon, hanging on you trustingly, but okay, it will even give you a kind of seduction.

Horrific nightmare stories

Horror stories about him what a word is this horror dog that confirms that you are not okay and there is something scary for you

coming out of the dark to make sure that you are afraid to sniff your fear of me after the great smell of fear lovely

For some objects, the other can intimidate you and enjoy it, which demons can embrace and we take from horror stories to tell him that I met creatures from another world of this

A collection of some stories that I heard and decided on them and I remember them from childhood until now stuck in my head so often I read a lot of scary stories in every place online People's Health Council

This collection of his stories tells about a mission that happened in many places and still challenges you know what those goosebumps are that apply to your body when you hear stories about sexual demons if I bring

Camera while this chill is in the body of your photos and yourself, trust me if I find the photo we take, beware, there are pounds next to you, now read this story with you, see that you are not alone ...

Observers see this story now, and it is terrifying with stories about my modest pocket, you can demand that they be in my spare time I repeat the stories that you have collected from many places in different places on the Internet

House with the ghosts

Tales of my nightmare, terrifying in the first part

One evening there was someone when one of his friends, who was on one of the days of Eid al-Adha, and when he was consistent with his friends, he played, and this includes their songs.

Save forgot your home far from them, and you have to lengthen and send early, but unfortunately, our friend, who are attracted by his songs and celebration, and I have to go now, because his house is too far, he will pass one of

Deserted roads, abandoned, along which not only cars transport big, but also very small ones, while he is having fun with his friends, one dirty clock on the wall looks at me, only to discover that the past

One after midnight today will not pass me by best of all, he knew it because his car gives so much friend decided we apologized finally he asked his friends to leave because it takes very data no go down to the car to quickly go down a little before like Fajr Azan was driving our friend his car while it was on the way it was discovered that the temperature of his car had risen, and get from the intensity of heat and all that.

Due to the lack of water in the radiator of his car, he parked his car in the middle of the road, and he was so damn scared because the road was dark and there were no street lamp posts, because this is a deserted road that was abandoned by the state, because it is not that important a lot, but his fear seemed to disappear when I found one of the shops that opened its doors at this time, cars were special.

Hair is our friend, I was lucky at last and I went in a hurry to buy him a bottle of water, entered the store and found a guy who looks like he is too old for people, his white face was standing against the wall and was counting the money, he said No

I want a bottle faster and so that the man's face can be found and our friend, a man with one eye, just entered our friend in a state of hysteria and severe horror and quickly headed to the car and despite the fact that her temperature soared to heaven and the next day our friend Lester returned about what happened to her and closed and when I asked one of the people said no in a closed store many years ago he killed this man.

In my hands one of the thieves stole his money, just look, but the door seems to be closed and it has been open since time immemorial and said that she knew who I met there

Sex shared party

Tales of my nightmare, terrifying in the first part

At that time, there was one of a group of young and careless people who, having returned to visit one of the mountain states, gave the rest to the people, they brought with them a number of flutes and drums to give a concert there

And the fire was lit and the party was loud and there was no sound, just the bodice of their voice that rises in the darkness of the mountains and they danced and sang and they had flutes and drums, probably a situation they described as amazing but in the desert you have to respect the office, even if it was free, maybe there is something that you do not see the tasks, as they sing and dance if someone else is available to them.

And they don't know where this stranger came from and where this stranger came from, told them please, my car broke down on the road and there are no stores here, I hope that you approved the network in your policy, but they said no, please, you will finish the party we attended at our party, please, I don't belong, and then go kill the man from the fire, what I feel is like this, but the strange man was, the features are not visible.

Half of the face is dark and the other half is pale; this man did not sleep a hundred years ago, did not care about him so much and threw a party while these two were dancing; the man looked strangely at the fact that it was he who treated them with the hand of the D person and said

Someone please forward my interests with some scratches has not a single incomplete person to talk to him and friends and they found him very hairy, with hooves like going out if their cry screams

Loudly and in every place of horror, imagine a dark place by the cries of a person who does not know its source and where it comes from, someone needs help, they say that after that they did not find the net again.

He also says that he found their lifeless bodies, and they found them too, but they need crazy curiosity about this story that happened in one of the mountainous regions of an Arab

Cat street poor

Tales of my nightmare, terrifying pocket part one

While someone sits at home in one of the old quarters and a bitch that was built a long time ago, sitting on one of the cold nights, reading a book or a newspaper, in the evening they return to stay very much and the atmosphere

Suitable for the sky it is raining now, and very cool I almost feel that the cold would tear my limbs went to sleep finally cooler and Linda of some kind of defense looked out the window, he finds that the dispute go to suicide because of the harsh air and very windy and the sky is changeable and controlled at the beginning of sleep I heard the doorbell ring badly and one of them wants to bother me I sleep to do if mine was hit by a product to get a cat.

The little girl, wet from the rain, standing by the door and meowing to me with her voice, was not really thinking about how the wound cat rings the doorbell, but about how she looks and how her body is thin and says that she needs to pay. and food cannot leave her. this animal and compassion to her home to tell her some food and drink and dry her body from the rain water he had no matter if she was carrying fleas or not to save her

The spirit does not need justification and the need to sacrifice it seemed that she was eating food greedily and she did not see that the food was in the trash bins there is a street that is the source of livelihood sector of the streets it does not matter let her into the house and went to sleep turned off the light and left her to sleep in the living room, it is dark warm when I fell asleep I began to think about the ringing of the bell at the door, but soon they are in deep sleep in the second hour after

In the middle of the night, I woke up to satisfy my needs. I went to the bathroom and found a cat sitting in the darkness and silence around, she looked at me, and her smile gave me goose bumps, but I was on my own, and in the morning, when dawn broke, winter had already stopped and the clouds began to give donations, went to the cat and said that this time I had to leave, I grabbed her, opened the door and put her on the floor, and I said goodbye, but I had to be horrified when I saw her smiling face.

Smile broadly and tell me that I have her tongue Thank you, a generous person will forget what you did to me was amazingly fast no creature was so fast terrible it was her fly, as lightning say that after a person walked into a dirty bird, seeing a cat smiling at him.

Decide not to choose

Tales of my nightmare, terrifying pocket part one

Once upon a time there was a family of two sisters, and the daughter of Abu Dhabi was a younger sister sleeping next to a large bed, one was the older sister of a mentally ill, but not driven to madness

She spoke normally, but with the same complex ideas she is crazy and behaves violently, but she loved her sister very little, and one day gloomy went to bed and went to her younger sister to sleep next to her older sister, and she looked at her younger sister for more than half an hour who was next to her on the bed to make her look at her as a very scary smiling asset management girl.

The small face of the pleura from the severity of horror and horror, and if it can again turn into its natural and dormant weak girl, it will soon forget what happened, because, of course, small and all that

Water is just a game and entertainment, but the next day she slept the girl next to her older sister again and what happened, but after a deep sleep and found that her sister was looking at her again the same system and the same smile, But the girl this time , I screamed and strongly through her struggle continued to attack my older sister, and she tries to muffle her breathing, she says, the voice is very homely, this is not her voice, shut up, you know that it is not so

Mom and Dad who came in also made me bother and broke down the door, but, unfortunately, I found myself too late to kill the big and the little one, strangled her at Mom and Dad, amazed at how it happened. this ... this looks like her sister.

How they caught the big house and they said No why did you do this to my daughter so sure after I caught her and beat her because she killed her little sister and she told them it bothered me honestly expected it, but even after the period was summoned by one of the elders to tell the girl about me and I went angrily embarrassing him to tell her little sister because she bothered him so much, to be honest, more appropriate

Can genies and ghosts kill you ?!

Not so long ago, it was decided to move the workshop of our work to a new place, the tenant rented a large house (villa) in the area, which was once the habitat of the families of the rich members of the velvet, but these have long since left the country due to war conditions, their ruins remained empty except for the croaking of the crow and the never prowling that roams the gardens, the singing switched to the lonely jungle. Before leaving, he told us that army ghosts were roaming the house, said that mysterious voices were heard from the basement at night, and warned them never to go down, so as not to lose these voices, and as for the room on the second floor, he said that each of the costumes that appear in the zones of a crazy woman, her clothes are dirty, her hair is fluffy, her gaze is wandering, approaching a person sleeping with an ironic laugh, you first tickle his feet, then suddenly pull at the toe of his boot. his great full force tends to get scared, discovering he's already painted on his bed! ...

Are ghosts capable of killing you ?!
Crazy woman knocks you off your feet ..

What a story, it's not a secret for anyone who got up to hear it, I'm not so much at the place of work as in the perception that I live in a new house and say things like: what will this do to you? ... And here I am not talking about a normal house, but about a villa with an area of more than a thousand meters, where vast gardens are located in a quiet area.

Maybe you will feel a lot of fear during the day, but when night falls, bringing darkness with you, while leaving all the staff in closets, corridors, in the voids of black, dressed in what I don't know, only God, and while camping absolute silence on everything except the rustle of the trees whispering grasshopper, we are a female partner somewhere in the garden, when you intensified your worries and even smiled at you and thought.

The new ruler, a young man of enormous build, his name is Ahmad, took on the color of his complexion when I heard this story, but he showed us courage and composure and in vain said that the old guard was unhappy inevitably because of leaving him to their deed this story to tell us.

Thank God that I did not spend a day alone in this house, it was decided to transfer me to another place. But after a while the coincidence of the guard and A. I eagerly asked him about the product and is it really haunted? According to him, he left the building in this house after two months did not hear any strange sounds and saw a crazy woman in towels, but throughout this period it was necessary to obsessively with the annoying presence of something invisible leaving him and watching him on the ground. it's like sitting somewhere with the feeling that someone is happening to you a lot, but in case A. Where you paint around it, there were only valve walls. Most of all he is afraid, he says that this awakening from sleep scared him more than once, and every time he feels that someone nearby is vigorously shaking him, as if he wants to wake him up, but when he opens his eyes and does not find anyone next to him in room.

The story of the case of A. is the most outlandish of the frightening, this is the end, I did not see or hear anything unusual, the only abnormal thing was him, are there really ghosts in the house? Or that the whispers and doubts that arise from the perception of his progress through the house are accepted as appropriate in his bed? ... I mean, when you live in a house that you call haunted, you will involuntarily feel the pressure that will change things that may not have a real existence and may require its sinister, just as happened with the young English Assembly Charisse Glenn - 18 years old - who moved from her family home in the heart of English Leeds to Cornwall to be close to her friends, found a job as a waitress in a local bar and rented a small apartment.

Are ghosts capable of killing you ?!
Charissa Glenn

Everything went well with Karissa, she is happy with her life and her new and loved by everyone, that a rainy day came that day, which I heard from one of her friends or neighbors, that there is a young girl who lived in her apartment before committed suicide by hanging herself in the bathroom. This story was not signed by Thunderbolt on Karissa, it amazed her. embittered her life, and she had a feeling of overwhelming and there is a ghost or essence of ease to live with her in an apartment, watching nightmares became a routine part of her dreams, so she called her mother three times in one week seeing girls in neighborhoods every night!.

The mother told her daughter to leave the rented apartment for another, she said that she would pay the rent instead of her, the mother should have been afraid for her daughter, especially when she found out that Karissa was suffering from walking problems while sleeping, a sign that she was a nerd type, etc. But Karissa did not leave the apartment.Unfortunately, she probably did not find an alternative apartment in the neighboring area, and every day her fears and apprehensions grew, and she even told her sister that she began to often return to her apartment when she finished work at night.

Of course, some will say that Karissa's risk is not in place, but that it's just whispers and negative feelings stemming from the story about the girl in her apartment, and that if you don't hear this story, she will never be blacked out. Because he had already heard about the area being haunted, and I bet anyone would feel comfortable and would not close their eyes if they knew that someone died a terrible death in his house. But the course of Karissa's story backwards is bizarre in relation to something just beyond whispering and worrying ... one chilly November morning in 2008, I didn't bring Karissa to her work as usual, and didn't respond to all of her family and friends' contacts. .. what happened to him? Nobody knows that.

Finally, when urgently her parents went to some of her colleagues in her apartment to ask about her, they knocked on the door several times without an answer, they decided to open the door, forcibly entered, they went around the whole apartment until they found Karissa, she was in the bathroom, dead, committed suicide, wrapped a pink scarf over her shower and hung herself! ...

That's a coincidence? ... Does it make sense to hang two young girls yourself in the same way in the same place. Here you see that the risks of Karissa's nightmares, she interacted with sleep problems when he pushed her to unconsciously commit suicide, and you confirm that this dog is the one that the company did not default, in your records you indicate the occurrence of an accident, the suicide of a young girls in the apartment where Karissa used to live. While others felt that the apartment was probably actually haunted, and the ghosts of the apartment you cannot Charissa only after fear began to notice it, creatures that specifically feed on fear, the more you fear them the more they becoming prey easier for him and that's exactly what happened to Charisse, these objects are hidden I got him and buried him in the end to end my life by hanging myself in the bathroom.

But to impose the health of the last glance, understanding, the question arises: Are the objects special, capable of harming you? to what extent murder? ...

Are there ghosts that can kill you ?!
She can kill you if she wants to, directly or indirectly,

Some kind of spiritual answer: yes, they say that these items can kill you, if she wants, directly or indirectly, a way to pay you as a high-rise place or help your heart before a heart attack or open electrical contact, turns on the fire in your room while you sleep, etc. Form the gas directly to it, paying you to kill yourself, as the influence on your mind and your thoughts even makes you hallucinate and kill yourself. You may think, dear reader, that this is impossible, but personally close to me, he stabbed himself with a knife, he thought that someone was chasing him, and for many years he treated him just as practically useless, he always tried to commit suicide, therefore they hid all the knives in the house for him, but one day when his family was there, it seems he found a knife, he stabbed himself, put his head over the sink, then cut his own throat, even his hand is unable to carry the knife, fell plopping into his blood until he died.

Some may say that this is a psychological case and has nothing to do with the party, etc. shit, maybe they were right, but this world is clearly not filled with true stories, the related parts are stranger than just mental disorders and mental crises emergency. Let me give you a sample of them, with confirmation that this story is documented in the company's records and written about its health, which I did not leave my parental home.

Are ghosts capable of killing you ?!
Paul Carroll

Let's take the first story of tomorrow's birthdays in 2014. Paul was Carol sitting in the foyer of his house in Constance English and he feels weary and harsh as he talks exaggeratedly emotionally and learned about his eye-signed coincidence on the Ouija board was his daughter who bought her, to hang out with his friends, Paul decided to entertain himself with a game of the Ouija board. For those who do not know what the Ouija board is and says that it is a wooden board of a rectangular relief lettering of the alphabet, you can communicate with ghosts by moving your wooden pointer over letters to form words, and they say that their source is another world ... Or rather, this is what worries his believers in the possibilities of this onboard demon.

According to Paul, codified by the police, he was able to contact what appeared to be an evil spirit, but that spirit was accepted during the meeting and reflected in the dog's body for the Molly family! ... How it happened and how Paul found out that the soul entered the dog .. I don't know .. maybe the pronunciation of the word spoke to him, the important thing is that Paul was afraid to take Molly's dog to the bathroom, drown her in the bathtub, and then he cut it open her body was part of speech in a gutter that existed near his house, which, of course, led to the clogging of the drain, so the orderlies opened them the next day and soon they found the remains of a dog inside it. It seems that one of the disgruntled Pavel's neighbors called the police and told them about the reality of finding the dog's body, he was arrested and accused of cruelty to animals and sentenced to turn off the alarm.

Here, maybe, the story does not look so strange, despite the fact that a person drowns his dog and body, because Copper's spirit is where there is a lot of strange and crazy, but the story does not end there, we are still in our helmsman the wheelhouse, which is the strangest thing ..

Are ghosts capable of killing you ?!
Margaret and Katrina Carroll, shaped by them scarier than sex!

In the next world, tomorrow and at Christmas too, I decided for Paul's wife Margaret to play Ouija with her youngest daughter Katherine on the very board that paid her husband to have the world of the past kill his dog, and the ill-fated board already brought here played and they seem to have successfully communicated with a spirit from another world, I downloaded a very depressing message to their spirit, I tell them that both of you will die very soon.

What happened the next day seems confusing in fact, when the solution in the evening brought Margaret all in the prescription pill area, mixed them together, and then cracked down on her daughter before passing out from mother and daughter, setting parts of the region on fire to to ensure their death, I mean, if the drive does not kill them, there will be their fire. But God disappointed the others, my male children, they were able to save the mother, and her daughter was transferred to the hospital in critical condition. They were later tried on charges of vandalism and sentenced each to four years.

What do you think about this story now? If you still insist on this psychological position, let me introduce you to the story of another, more exotic one.

One evening in 2001, in a small town, quiet and calm from Lincoln County to the United States, Carol Sue, who replaced her grandmother, was a guest at her daughter Tammy's house, while her grandfather and his daughter and granddaughter were sitting at the door of the mall, playing Ouija sessions. At first everything seemed normal, her four children and leaving on Friday were strange and the concept that they received from the panel, but quickly changed the course of events, suddenly the granny was driven crazy, ran into the kitchen and returned with a big knife, then went to the next one her daughter's husband Briar, who was sleeping there, stabbed her in the chest, I stabbed him with a bang, he must die, because an evil spirit entered his body, Brian continued to scream and bleed until he died. Let us dwell on the fact that, having killed the wife of her daughter, the grandson of her little ten-year-old attacked her grandmother and tried to kill her other, claiming that an evil spirit had taken over her body, but Tammy's daughter managed to take the knife away from her and hide it.

Are ghosts capable of killing you ?!
Grandmother crashed into a car in an attempt to kill the family.

A few hours later, the grandmother with her son and grandson left the house and went by car, maybe she wanted Tamila to transfer her mother to the hospital in order to control the crazy surprise, but the grandmother insisted that you were a car and quickly tried to kill everyone with a control blow on purpose to one of the traffic lights on the highway, but, fortunately, the daughter and granddaughter survived from two minor injuries, and the woman was a grandmother, broke her ankles, but this did not prevent her from trying to kill her big granddaughter, five to ten VIA springs dragged her and pushed her towards the highway in the hope that it will run over it. A car rushed past, and then fell into a traffic jam, ran away, I ran and jumped over the consequences of the highway like a gazelle, although I broke my ankle! ... She looked more like justice in the green youth of the old fifties, and finally, to complete the food madness, she stripped off all her clothes, and then trotted towards the forest located on the side of the road and disappeared there.

The police found my grandmother the next day, and she was all rolled up under a large tree stump in the woods and was taken to the hospital.

This is a story that is not subject to the logic of surprised and perplexed everyone, someone might think that the crime is probably related to family problems, sexual harassment or domestic violence, but the police did not find any indication of the existence of differences and problems in the family. and there was no reason to pay the old man for the murder of her husband, her daughter and try to kill the grandson of two daughters, and all the friends and relatives of the family said that they were from their grandmother as a completely normal woman who did not go through a single psychological crisis in her life and did not smoked and did not drink alcohol or not. use drugs.

What happened next? .. What is the motivation for her crime? .. When you ask her about it during her trial, the old grandmother said that God told her to do it, and when she was playing on the Ouija board and I heard a voice resonating in her head, ordering them to kill Brian and the granddaughter, because that an evil spirit entered their bodies.

What do you think now? ... Whether the same or more objects present are actually capable of harming humans, for your information, similar stories occur in all parts of the world, and the layout of the rippled realism nightmare of experiments that talk about the demon and the physical and psychological harm that can be done to humans because of sex, ghosts and goblins.

But here the question arises: why do you say that the world offends other people? ..

The answer is this: for a variety of reasons, people often harm themselves through the practice of magic or by trying to get to the doors of another world with the help of some games of satanic nature.

Are there ghosts that can kill you ?!
Popular beliefs I doused myself with hot water harmed sex

Sometimes the motivation is revenge, there is such a widespread belief in our countries that pouring hot water into the shower or hitting a dog with a dough on the wall or with a stake in the ground without registration, any statement in the name of Allah, compassionate, merciful, can lead to big trouble. as far as sex is concerned, these beliefs are not the limit of the Covenant; they are rooted in the past, they believed the Arab side that sex can kill people, the most famous were those who argued that sex kills him is a war on illiteracy. Before that, thousands of years, people believed in ancient Egypt of the Mesopotamian valley that the souls of the dead, not ghosts, it can return from the other world to ensure that the living are haunted, this evil often manifests itself as a form of human illness, in the sense that they think that most diseases caused by the meeting of evil spirits, especially those spirits that prevent people from dying horribly, like victims of murder, or those who have never found their bodies, cards. These old beliefs still exist in one form or another in most parts of the Earth, leaving people of the East and West to believe in the existence of evil ghosts, these are the spirits of people who tragically died killed or suicidal, or maybe they died unjustly, so their lives bitter and seeking revenge. This design existed among the Arabs, and since they believed that the spirit of a deceased person would turn into a bird known as critical or important to stay hovering around the grave of its owner, he exclaims: "ARE ... ARE". and stop yelling until it counts.

Adoration can be a motive for harming people with the help of hidden objects, according to popular beliefs there are beings from another world who fall in love with men and women of us and theirs, and this love can require physical contact, often without the desire or consent of the side of the media, i.e. it acts like rape. Of course, some people scoff at these things shows that they exist in the company only because of sexual repression and emotional deprivation, but this is a misperception, the history of sex is public in all parts of the globe, and you can write (Incubi and succubi) the search engine will be a lot of many stories and experiences that are foreign to what we call us in the world - and a return to comprehensive about that.

Are there ghosts that can kill you ?!
Moore's family home inhabited in the archives

Finally, a person's problems with objects of the other world can be associated with their trading world, it is known that ghosts use parts of the private, houses, abandoned places where negative energy is great, it can act hostilely towards people who are trying to live in the same the same place, understanding the prospect of generating income for clients, it is like having someone whom you do not know your line to live in spite of you in your house or apartment. what will be your reaction? .. "will the mind, of course, continue to behave cruelly, thus, living in enchanted places will sometimes have serious consequences, psychologically and physically, especially if the object of metaphysics dwells in those places of a hostile and evil nature, and that the consequences will strike not only for ordinary people, but even for those people who claim to be professional in communicating with objects of the world around them another case of ghosts who see them on TV shows, as happened with a ghost hunter? American Robert Stephen, who visited one of the houses, famous for being haunted, this white wooden old house is located in a very small town called my visa in Iowa, Home witnessed a heinous crime committed one night in 1912, where the owner of the house, Mr. Josiah Moore, was killed, his wife Sarah, their four children, to add to the two children who were visiting the family, they were all killed with an ax, and the law will never accept that she The history of this murder has been preserved by investigators and researchers for decades - it will still return to the future. Robert decided to spend the night in this haunted house in 2014 to investigate his alleged ghosts, and at about 1 pm after midnight - God knows why - stabbed himself in the chest, wondering if the time of the strike coincided with the time of the crime in this region for more than a hundred years. What's even funnier is that when I searched for sources for this article, I discovered that there are other ghost bounty hunters, they are married couple Mark and Debbie Constantino, spent time in this region also in 2014, so that eventually after a few months to be dead, where Mark killed his wife and then shot himself.

www.ingramcontent.com/pod-product-compliance
Lightning Source LLC
Chambersburg PA
CBHW061539120726
48001CB00004B/1623